CALIFORNIA GIRL

Why is he looking at me? I kept asking myself. This cafeteria is full of girls. And he is so good looking himself...

I took another quick peek at him. The first thing I noticed about him had been the longish dark hair, but now I saw his eyes. They were looking straight at me.

Pull yourself together Jennie, I lectured myself. Be reasonable. You know he's only staring at you because he's heard that you're a weirdo who goes to swim at five in the morning and never goes to parties..

Bantam Sweet Dreams Romances
Ask your bookseller for the books you have missed

P.S. I LOVE YOU by Barbara P. Conklin
LITTLE SISTER by Yvonne Greene
LAURIE'S SONG by Suzanne Rand
PRINCESS AMY by Melinda Pollowitz
CALIFORNIA GIRL by Janet Quin-Harkin
THE POPULARITY PLAN by Rosemary Vernon

California Girl

Janet-Quin Harkin

BANTAM BOOKS
TORONTO · NEW YORK · LONDON · SYDNEY

RL 5, IL age 11 and up

CALIFORNIA GIRL

A Bantam Book/September 1981

Sweet Dreams is a Trademark of Bantam Books, Inc.

Cover photo by Ariel Skelley.

ISBN 0-553-20324-X

Published simultaneously in the United States and Canada

Bantam Books are published by Bantam Books, Inc. Its trademark, consisting of the words "Bantam Books" and the portrayal of a bantam, is Registered in U.S. Patent and Trademark Office and in other countries. Marca Registrada. Bantam Books, Inc., 666 Fifth Avenue, New York, New York 10103.

PRINTED IN THE UNITED STATES OF AMERICA

0 9 8 7 6 5 4 3 2 1

Chapter 1

The hum of the air conditioner in the cafeteria was so loud it almost drowned out the conversation below it—and with several hundred kids all talking at once, that was a pretty noisy air conditioner. It also didn't work very well. If you sat on one side of it, it missed you completely, and you sweated. If you sat directly in front of it, it was like being at the North Pole.

I happen to hate air conditioners. I have this theory that they can actually suck all the air *out* of a room. Someday I'll be in a room with one, and I won't be able to breathe anymore. I hate rooms without windows, too. I suppose it is because I was brought up in California and was used to big windows and lots of fresh air. Anyway, I felt like a prisoner, trapped in this big, windowless room while the air conditioner hummed at me from the ceiling and hundreds of kids yelled at one another all around me.

As I looked around, it seemed that everyone else in the whole cafeteria was busy talking and laughing. Everyone else was sitting with their friends. I was the only one who knew nobody and sat alone like Cinderella in the corner. This was how it had been every lunchtime since we moved to Texas.

Even my food didn't seem to taste good anymore, and that is saying a lot. If there is one thing in the world that I like to do, it is eat. The words "poor appetite" never were in my vocabulary up to now. But in that cafeteria my sandwiches tasted like cardboard.

I would have preferred to eat outside in the shade of the pine trees, even if it was ninety-five in the shade and humid out there. But when I asked a teacher if I could eat outside, he looked as if I had asked for permission to take off all my clothes. Students were never permitted to eat on the grass, he said. After all, they littered the place with Coke cans and sandwich wrappers and never cleaned up after themselves. I got the feeling that if he had his way, he would ban students from high school altogether and just have a nice, clean, empty building.

I couldn't help thinking back to lunchtime in California. A group of us, mostly kids from my swim team, took our lunches out to eat on the grass. There was this big eucalyptus tree, and we used to lie in the shade. It always smelled so good—of eucalyptus and pine and other clean smells. Some days we used to talk and laugh. Other days we would just lie back and look up at the blue sky through the eucalyptus leaves or watch the hills in the distance.

Suddenly the memory was too much for me to bear. I switched it off with an effort of willpower. I seemed to be spending my whole life thinking, "In California we always used to..." In fact, that was fast becoming my most-used phrase in the English language. I'll make an effort not to use it so much—it becomes boring after a while.

For a moment I felt like crying. I felt my eyes start to sting, and I rubbed them quickly, without thinking. Then I remembered that I had probably smeared my mascara. I never wore mascara in California, so I wasn't used to not rubbing my eyes.

Now I probably look more freaky than ever, I thought gloomily.

I always got depressed around lunchtime. Having nobody to sit with in the cafeteria was only part of it. The trouble was that lunch period was always the time I was most tired. Because of swimming practice, I had already been up and working for almost eight hours by lunchtime. When you looked at it that way, it just didn't seem fair. If I were an adult and belonged to a union and people wanted me to work that many hours, we'd all go on strike. Unfortunately I couldn't go on strike, and I was only halfway through my day. The afternoon seemed to stretch out endlessly ahead of me.

I had more classes, and they were chemistry and social studies, my two most unfavorite classes. Then there was the bus ride home, surrounded by noisy, yelling, giggling, juvenile kids. That was followed by a quick snack and quick change, and then it was back to the pool for evening workout.

The evening workout was the tough one.

The early-morning workout was mainly to build our stamina. We swam thousands and thousands of meters, sometimes with a kickboard, sometimes with pull buoys, sometimes without. I was now in my third year of morning workouts. I had learned how to wake up the part of me that was needed to get dressed, get me to the pool, and swim, while the rest of me stayed asleep. I found it quite possible to go up and down, my arms and legs moving mechanically, while the rest of me dozed in a comfortable, private daydream.

But the evening workout—that was different. That was all hard work. First, the half hour on the universal gym—a giant torture machine of weights and counterweights that had to be pulled, stretched, and lifted by all parts of the body in turn. Then another two hours in the pool working on timed intervals—so many hundreds on the one-ten, then so many two hundreds, so many fifties. And my coach was so considerate—"Jennie, do yours all fly," he would say. "The rest of you do yours freestyle." I happen, unfortunately, to be a butterflyer. People say it is the toughest, most demanding stroke. Some days I agree. I have asked myself many times why I couldn't have been a natural breaststroker. I ask myself that usually when I am coming down the twentieth length of butterfly and am trying to drag my aching body clear of the water.

I can remember very clearly the day when I first met Tod Milner, my coach. I was nine years old, and my mother had enrolled me in a stroke clinic. We were all beginners, and the coach had just taught us how to do the butterfly. The other kids all thrashed and gasped their way across the pool, but I just seemed to wiggle my whole body, and I reached the other side with no effort at all. At that moment Tod happened to come by. He called me over and asked my name. He was big and blond. To little nine-year-old me, he looked like some sort of god. When he smiled, his eyes sort of crinkled. "You are a natural flyer, young lady," he said. "I'd like to talk to your parents about you."

I suppose I ought to mention that my mother had been a champion swimmer. She almost made the Olympics. But she was on this date with my father when they had a car crash, and so she couldn't make the trials. So after Tod met my parents and found out who my mother was, nobody was surprised that I was a natural flyer—except me. I was surprised that I was naturally anything, except clumsy. I was always tall and skinny for my age and always seemed to trip over my own feet. In fact, when we had to pick teams at school, I was usually the last one picked. After I had gotten over my surprise, I felt good to be a natural something. I liked having big kids make a fuss over me and having Tod as my coach. Much to everyone's surprise, he took me straight to his own group with all the seniors. I got so used to hearing people discuss my "peaking in time for the Olympics" that it seemed quite normal to me.

I couldn't really remember a time when Tod was not part of my life. He was a real slave driver, pushing me on and on when I thought I was going to die. But he only had to smile that crinkle-eyed smile of his, and I would work twice as hard to please him. He became as much a part of my life as eating and breathing.

One thing he did was to enter into a plot with my mother. "Don't worry, Mrs. Webster, we'll get her to the Olympics for you," he told her once, and from then on they worked as a team.

"Doesn't Tod want you to go to bed early this week?" my mother would ask.

"Doesn't your mother expect you to wear your hat after practice in this weather?" Tod would say.

Big Brother and Big Sister watching over me twenty-four hours a day. In California I hadn't thought much about things. But then in California I had friends and family and not much time to myself to sit and think. In Texas I had too much time to myself and thought too much. I began to wonder if I was a person at all, or just a machine programmed to swim fast. It was scary how everything had changed, as if the world had tilted suddenly. Back in California, swimming was an OK thing to do. Most kids had been on a swim team at some time in their lives, and the other kids at school thought that winning the Junior Nationals was a pretty neat thing to do. They didn't worship me or think I was Superwoman or anything. They understood, though, that I had to spend most of my life training and the rest of it sleeping, eating, and competing. But Texas, that was another story. . . .

A group of girls walked past my table toward the door of the cafeteria. I recognized two of them. The two blonds were Tracy Reinhard and Marylee Cox. They were both Golden Girls—that's what the cheerleaders were called at Oak Creek High. The other girls were either cheerleaders or admirers. The Golden Girls walked as if they knew everyone was watching them. Their walk seemed to say, "Don't you wish you were me!" They looked just like cheerleaders were supposed to look. They wore tight jeans with the right labels on the back and satiny blouses or tight T-shirts with low necklines, which showed off very curvy figures underneath. They had carefully made-up faces with perfect teeth, wide, blue doll eyes with long mascaraed lashes, and long, heavy manes of hair, feathered back, curled with a hot brush away from their faces, so clean and silky that it bounced up and down as they walked.

In spite of the fact that I would rather die than be a cheerleader, I couldn't help feeling a bit jealous of them. When you have a figure that is straight up and down and even slim-cut jeans won't stay up over your hips, it would certainly be nice to have a few curves. My father tells me kindly that I am a late developer and that I'll surprise everybody one day. But then my father is always the kindhearted one, so I expect he is just trying to make me feel good. My mother, the practical one, tells me that I can thank my lack of figure for my good swimming times. She's right, of course. My mother is nearly always right. There was this girl in California who used to be my main competition in the hundred fly. Then suddenly around thirteen she developed this large bust and quietly dropped out of swimming. Being flat-chested may be good in my chosen sport, but still, I would give a lot for a few curves in the right places.

I would give a lot for the Golden Girls' hair. My own hair is just blah. I bet if you asked anyone who knew me to describe my hair, they wouldn't be able to. It covers the top of my head. That's about all you can say for it. I wear it as short as possible because I can't stand cold, wet hair dripping down my back when I get out of the pool in the winter. Its color could be described most kindly as mid-brown. In California it did get nice blond highlights from all that sun. I think I might look good blond. I did try to use a lightener on it once, but it turned green after three days of chlorine.

I had better mention at this stage that I do not have perfect teeth, wide blue eyes, or a cute little snub nose, either. Once when I was feeling depressed about my face, my father told me that I had an interesting face and that Sophia Loren was not a perfect beauty, either. This didn't help too much since most people my age don't know Sophia Loren from Adam. Sometimes I think that my eyes are my one good feature. They are halfway between blue and green. If I wear my favorite blue sweater they look blue, and with my team warm-up jacket they are clearly green. At least it's nice to have eyes that match your wardrobe.

As the Golden Girls passed me, I heard one of them say, "That's the one who—" I lost the end of the sentence, but I could guess what she was saying because the other girls turned around and stared as if I were an exhibit in a museum. I felt myself blushing, but I don't suppose they noticed. They had already lost interest and were walking away. But one of them had a loud voice. I heard it clearly.

"You wouldn't think it to look at her, would you?" she said. "She doesn't have big muscles."

"She doesn't have big anything!" another said. They all collapsed in giggles as they went through the swinging doors.

I don't ever remember feeling more helpless and defenseless. How I longed for some way to prove my worth to them. But I knew it was useless. Even if I won the Olympics, these girls wouldn't think I was hot stuff. Hot stuff was looking like them and being a Golden Girl and dating a football player. Outside of those things, nothing else mattered. Little Jennie Webster, who dated nobody, was a great big zero.

I stared for a while at the cafeteria door, trying to stop feeling angry and foolish and homesick and miserable. Then I got the feeling that someone was watching me. I looked quickly to the right, and it was true. The area to the right of the doors was in a shadow—the lighting being as useless as the air conditioner. In that shadow a dark-haired boy was sitting and looking at me. I glanced around quickly to make sure he was really looking at me . . . not at some gorgeous blond sitting right behind me. I was all alone. Then I stared down hard at my half-eaten sandwich and wished more than ever for long hair so that I could let it hang across my face and peer at the boy without his knowing I was watching him. I could feel him still looking at me. He looked at me all the time I chewed my cheese and lettuce sandwich, all the time I chewed my ham and tomato sandwich, and all the time I chewed my apple. I had never really thought much about chewing before, but now I realized how stupid people look with their jaws going up and down.

"Why is he looking at me?" I kept asking myself. "This cafeteria is full of girls. And he is so good-looking, too." I took another quick peek at him. The first thing I had noticed about him had been the longish, dark hair, but now I saw his eyes. They were looking straight at me—beautiful large, dark eyes, fringed with lashes that were wasted on a boy. I only glanced for a moment. But even in that short time, I saw that his eyes looked deep and haunting and very sad. He had the sort of face you might see on a painting in an art gallery or on an actor playing Hamlet or on a poet. It was a handsome face, but in some way out of place in Oak Creek High School, Texas.

"Pull yourself together, Jennie," I lectured myself. "Be reasonable. You know he's only staring at you because he's heard that you're a weirdo who swims at five o'clock every morning and never goes to parties."

I had finished my lunch and had no excuse to keep sitting there. Besides, I had to get to my locker before class. I couldn't help walking close to his table. Just to see if he said anything to me, just in case he didn't think I was a freak. . . .

As I got closer my heart started beating so loudly I expected people to look up to see where the noise was coming from. But of course they didn't. Nobody noticed me at all. I walked down the line of benches, past all the chatting kids, down to the very end where the dark-haired boy was sitting.

He was no longer looking at me. He was looking down instead. I had planned to sweep past him looking poised and busy, but, of course, being me, I was only one pace away when I tripped over something. I put out my hand to stop myself from falling, and of course, again being me, I knocked a pile of papers off the table. They fluttered to the floor. I was crimson with embarrassment by this time. I mumbled something and bent to pick them up. Then I froze with my hand on the first paper. It was a beautiful pencil sketch, and it was of me!

My eyes rose to meet the boy's. "Is this yours?" I asked, and I heard my voice tremble.

He nodded and took it back from me. "You were an interesting subject to draw," he said. "I hope you don't mind."

"You draw very well. It looks just like me," I stammered.

"I have to be able to do one thing very well," he said, and I noticed that his voice was as dark and sad as his face. "Since lately I'm so useless at everything else."

Only then did I notice that what I had tripped over were his crutches.

Chapter 2

I couldn't stop thinking about him all day. I thought about what had happened after I had fallen over his crutches. I suppose someone less shy than I would have come right out and said, "Hey, what did you do to your leg?" But I couldn't. He obviously had felt embarrassed, too. He had mumbled something about being late for class and said he'd see me around sometime. Then he pulled himself to his feet and tucked his crutches under his arms. He gathered up his papers, including the sketch of me, and swung himself expertly toward the door. Some kid leaped up to open it for him. "There you go, Mark, old pal," he said as the boy went through.

I didn't know anybody in my chemistry or social studies classes well enough to ask them about him. To be honest, I didn't know anybody in my classes well enough to ask them anything. But I thought about him nonstop. In fact, both teachers picked on me for daydreaming. Mr. Schiffman, my chemistry teacher, had to ask me a question twice. Then he asked me sweetly if I intended to graciously bestow my full presence on the class for the rest of the period. All the kids who were smart enough to have that sort of vocabulary laughed. Then the others laughed, too, because it was better than doing chemistry.

After school I had to hurry out of the building because the school bus left right away. Then I had ten minutes at home to put on my swimsuit and grab a glass of milk and peanut-butter sandwich before my car pool came to pick me up. It was no use asking anyone in my car pool about the boy. My car pool was another big disappointment about Texas. In California, riding to swimming practice had been one of the best parts of the day. I used to ride with four boys. We spent the whole time teasing each other, laughing about what Tod had said to us that day, and making fun of other swimmers we had to swim against in meets.

"Remember your poor old buddies when you win the Olympics and get paid a million dollars to do a milk commercial," we used to kid each other.

But this new car pool was different. There were no other high-school kids in it. There were hardly any other high-school kids on the whole swim team. My car pool was made up of one girl from junior high named Lori Peterson and two little kids from the beginners group. Lori wasn't the least bit interested in swimming and never bothered to talk to me. The two little kids had heard a bit about me and looked at me as if I were a creature from Mars.

Our mothers took turns driving. This was

Mrs. Peterson's week, and I hated this one most. For one thing, Mrs. Peterson had white-blond hair, set like hair used to be in the fifties and sprayed stiff with hair spray. She kept the car windows shut and smoked cigarettes all the time, so my eyes were always watering by the end of the trip. Mrs. Peterson also thought that Lori was going to be a great swimmer. Why she ever thought that I couldn't imagine, because Lori was one of the most hopeless swimmers I had ever seen. She used to thrash her way up and down the pool, swinging her arms like windmills and holding onto the lane lines when she got tired. Although she was thirteen, she was in the lane reserved for the worst little kids. Even eight-year-olds got promoted out of that lane. But Mrs. Peterson would come and watch sometimes, and I would see her looking proudly at Lori.

At first I didn't see how Lori could stand being with all the little kids, but after a while I learned her secret. Most days Mrs. Peterson did not stay and watch. On those days Lori simply did not swim. She went into the shower and got her hair wet, to look like she had been swimming. Then she changed and went over to the drugstore to meet boys. On the way home Mrs. Peterson always asked Lori how she had done in swimming, and Lori always told her mother how hard she had worked. I always smiled to myself. It gave me a feeling of power to know that I had this good item of blackmail to hold over Lori if I ever needed it.

Lori hardly ever spoke to me in the car, but

Mrs. Peterson talked nonstop. She liked to talk about swimming, and she would usually ask me about my times. This was very embarrassing because she kept comparing me to Lori, and Lori was so bad.

That day she started in as soon as I climbed into the car. "Hello, Jennie. We were just having an argument about you. Do you really swim a hundred fly in under a minute? Lori said you did, but I said that couldn't be possible, since Lori takes almost two minutes."

Lori said nothing. Mrs. Peterson looked at me, waiting for an answer.

"Uh-huh," I said. In California there had been other kids who could do my times, but in this small new team I was labeled THE STAR, and everything I said sounded like bragging.

I tried to think of a way to change the subject, but Mrs. Peterson went right on. "My heavens," she said, "just think of that, Lori. Under a minute. That must be some sort of record, isn't it?"

"Not really," I said.

"She holds the Junior National record," Lori said. "Coach Milner told us." She gave me a sneer that said, "I know all about you, too."

That killed conversation for the rest of the trip. I was glad when Lori leaned over and switched on the radio to a loud rock station and I was left with my thoughts again. Who was that boy? Why was he on crutches? Why did he have to be so good-looking? Why, out of all the girls in the cafeteria, did he have to pick me to sketch? There seemed no way of ever finding out the answers.

Then suddenly it came to me—I remembered that I knew exactly who to ask about the boy. How could I have been so dumb and not thought of her before? After all, she was my next-door neighbor. Her name was Marilyn Porter, and she was also the world's number-one gossip.

Although she lived next door to me, we hadn't gotten to know each other very well for two reasons. First, she was everything my mother disapproved of in a teenager—she wore too much makeup and low-cut blouses and too-tight jeans. She drove her own car, too fast, and she was always arguing with her mother. She had come over with her mother the day we moved in. We we were standing in the middle of all our belongings, feeling lost and tired and ready to head straight back to California, when they came right in without knocking.

"I just knew y'all wouldn't have time to cook, so I brought you some chicken," Marilyn's mother had said. "I'm your neighbor, Marylou Porter, and this is Marilyn."

Marilyn leaned against the doorway and looked sulky. Mrs. Porter nudged her. "Say hi nicely, Marilyn."

"Hi nicely," said Marilyn in a cool voice.

Mrs. Porter shook her head. "She's at that difficult age." She sighed. "It's been really hard for me, now that I'm divorced. I have to work all day, and she's just been running wild. I don't know what to do with her—but then I guess all teenagers are the same."

"I don't know about that," said my outspoken mother. "I think the main thing is to keep them busy. My daughter Jennie spends so much time swimming that she doesn't have any energy left to get into trouble."

Marilyn looked at me as if I were a worm. Mrs. Porter's eyes lit up. "Oh, where does she swim?"

"She's going to join the team at the new swim center."

"Oh, how about that, Marilyn? You used to be on the team, didn't you? There was a swim team here that Marilyn was on, until it folded. She used to be quite good. I'd love her to take it up again. It's so good for them. So healthy—"

"So boring." Marilyn sighed.

"Perhaps you could take Marilyn along with you when your daughter goes, just so she could see what it's like," Mrs. Porter said.

I sighed inwardly at the thought of Marilyn being forced against her will to come to swim with me. I was sure she would hate every minute of it. But, funnily enough, it turned out quite differently. Marilyn was not in the least silent and sulky when her mother wasn't there, and she loved the swim team instantly.

"I'd forgotten about all those cute boys with the big shoulders," she said. "They all look so good in those little swim trunks."

This brings me to the second reason why I didn't see more of Marilyn. She was positively boy crazy. Every time I talked to her she told me all about her latest boyfriends. It didn't take me too long to figure out that most of the boyfriends were only in her mind. But she insisted on telling me every detail of what they said to her when they met in the halls at school, the notes they wrote her in class, and everything they did on their dates.

I couldn't believe that a quarter of those exciting things could have happened to an overweight, piggy-eyed girl like Marilyn. In fact, I had a suspicion that the best of her stories came straight from romance magazines. The one time I went over to her house, her room was full of *True Romance*, *Young Confessions*, and other similar magazines.

As soon as she had decided that the swim team had advantages and that I was the coach's favorite, she became very friendly with me. Being friendly meant telling me everything that went on in the entire school and at the swim center. I didn't know any of the people, so I didn't really care, and I soon got bored with Marilyn's confessions of her exciting dates.

As I had guessed, my mother let me know that Marilyn was not the sort of girl she wanted me to hang around with, and she wouldn't let me ride to swim practice in Marilyn's car. I can't say I was too sorry. Given a choice between Marilyn and the car pool, the car pool was probably the lesser of two evils. However, today was different. Today I could ask her about the boy at school, and she would be sure to know!

My thoughts were rudely jerked back to the present when Mrs. Peterson, who seemed to think of herself as a racing-car driver, swung the car around the circle at the South Texas

Swim and Athletic Center and screeched to a halt. We got out in silence and walked up the steps toward the main door. The center was a new, imposing structure of steel and glass, set amid the South Texas pines. It had been designed on a grand scale, no doubt for hosting future national or Olympic events, but as yet it had a half-empty look. This was because the local population had not yet grown to its predicted size and because the people who were here had not yet realized that there were other sports besides football. The swim team, the gymnastics team, and the diving team were just over a year old.

We walked through the main entry hall. On one side we could see little kids doing dangerous things on a balance beam in the main gym. On the other side some of the swim-team kids were already stretching in the weight room. We turned into the locker room just before the indoor pool. It was empty.

I didn't get a chance to speak to Marilyn before workout. She came late, as usual. She liked being on the swim team, but she didn't like to work, so she usually had some very good excuse as to why she was late, why she couldn't swim, or why she had to get out early. One day she had strained her finger lifting a book in the library. The next time someone had stepped on her big toe, or she had a cough, or her eyes were allergic to chlorine. They were very creative excuses, and I always enjoyed waiting to see what the next one would be. But today I was already hard at work when Marilyn slipped into the water.

The workout was a hard one, and Tod was in a bad mood. Tod always seemed to be in a bad mood these days. He hardly ever smiled anymore, just shouted and frowned. I had a good idea what the trouble was. In California he had been head coach of a big team. There were over two hundred kids, and he had two assistant coaches under him so he just worked with the best seniors. The offer to come to Texas and start this new team had been so fantastic that he couldn't refuse. They told him they wanted someone like him to build a national-class team. But the trouble was that the team did not yet exist. Most of the kids he had to work with at the moment would have been handed over to his assistants in California. These kids were like Marilyn, beginners or not very serious swimmers. I am sure he had asked himself more than once if the move had really been such a good idea.

What he did was put all his energy into coaching me, making sure that I, at least, kept up his reputation at the Nationals. What he didn't understand was that swimming was much harder for me here. We swam in the outdoor pool because it was Olympic size, and all summer the water had been much too warm. It made me feel tired and lazy. But that wasn't the main problem. Before, I had been one of a team. There had been a lot of friendly rivalry about who went first, who finished first. We had been rude to each other, grabbed each other's ankles, and had fun, as well as worked hard. Here I swam alone. I had a completely different workout from the rest of the kids. There was nobody to grab my heels if I slowed down, no one for me to beat in the sprints. I could tell the other kids thought I was some sort of stuck-up showoff and that they didn't think it was fair how much time Tod spent with me. I knew what they were thinking, but I didn't know what to do to make things better.

This afternoon Tod gave me even more attention than usual. But his temper was so bad that for once the other kids were glad he didn't notice them.

"What was that meant to be?" he yelled at me. "I said sprint, not fall asleep. I could have walked to Houston and back in the time that took you. Is this meant to be a swim team or a rehabilitation center for cripples? You had better crawl back to your crutches if that's the way you are going to swim."

The other kids all laughed. I think any other time I would have laughed, too. But now I knew someone who was on crutches, and I didn't find the remark funny. I felt angry, and I stormed my way down the next few lengths so fast that even Tod in his bad mood had to call, "That's more like it. You can really move if you want to."

After workout I hurried to catch Marilyn before she left. She had quit early as usual, having strained her back in gymnastics at school. She was already putting on her shoes when I came out dripping wet and sat down beside her.

"Terrible workout, wasn't it?" I said as I thumped down my bag.

She looked up and smiled at me. "Boy, I'll say. Coach Milner is one mean guy. I never met such a mean person. And he is really awful to you. If I were you, I would never have come all the way to Texas to be yelled at like that. I'd have stayed in California with all those cute, blond boys. I think I'm going to quit the team if he keeps on yelling like that. I mean, there aren't too many cute boys here, anyway. Did I ever tell you about the cute coach I used to have on a swim team? He liked me a lot. In fact, I nearly started dating him. He drove me home in his car after workout once. He had this really neat Porsche, but you know my mother. She came out and saw us. Boy, did she ever get mad! She won't ever let me date older guys. Anyway—"

"Marilyn, listen," I interrupted. When she started going on about how mean her mother was, it took just as long as telling me about her dates—and it was just as boring.

"Marilyn, I want to know about a boy at school."

"Oh, I know all the cute boys at Oak Creek," she said. "What's his name?"

"I don't know. He's dark with big dark eyes and very good-looking."

"Heeyyyyy," said Marilyn, licking her lips.

"And right now he's on crutches."

Marilyn's face fell. "Oh, him. You mean

Mark Waverly. He used to be such a cute guy till his accident."

"What happened to him—was he in a car crash?"

"Oh, no. He did it playing football. He used to be fantastic. You should have seen him run. There was no one who could catch him once he took off. Well, we were playing Lufkin for the championship, and these Lufkin guys all picked on Mark. They wanted to make sure he was out of the game, of course. That's the sort of dirty players they were. Well, the whole pack of them just fell on him and clobbered him real good. Oh, you should have seen how he looked when they carried him off the field. I thought I was going to throw up, honest I did. All the girls were crying—"

"Was he badly hurt?"

"Sure he was. He didn't get out of the hospital till spring. He did something to his back, I think, and smashed his kneecap. They thought for a while that he'd never walk again. Such a shame, he was a real cute guy."

"You mean he isn't cute anymore just because he got hurt and can't play football?" I asked angrily.

"Oh, no," Marilyn said quickly. "I didn't mean that at all. But he used to be real friendly and liked to joke and kid around, you know. But when he came back to school, he shut himself right away from other kids. As if he didn't want any friends anymore. You try talking to him, you'll see."

Chapter 3

When Mrs. Peterson's car pulled up outside our house, my father's car was already in the driveway. That was unusual. Most nights he complained that the traffic was horrible and said that he'd rather work late at the office than take his life in his hands with all those crazy pickup trucks. He was so worried about the millions of pickup trucks that he wouldn't let me drive at all, even though I had already passed drivers' ed. That was why I had to go on riding and suffering in the car pool.

With the big red Texas sun setting behind it, our house looked really pretty, like something out of a movie set. I got out of Mrs. Peterson's car and stopped in the driveway to stare at the house. I had to admit it was one of the plus points about moving. In California we had lived in a ranch-style house just like everyone else's—thirty houses all the same, all side by side on the same street. They were so alike that everyone kept their cornflakes in the cabinet to the right of the stove and had two fan palms in the front yard.

But houses were cheaper in Texas, and we

had been able to buy this beautiful brick house with balconies and pillars. It looked like something out of *Gone with the Wind*, and I always half-expected girls in hoop skirts to come running out. I opened the front door and went inside. The entrance hall was one of the most beautiful things about the house. It was marble with a big curved staircase and a chandelier. When we moved in, one of the neighbors said to my mother, "You'll just have to stay put in this house until your daughter gets married. Won't she make a beautiful bride, dressed all in white, coming down that staircase?"

I agreed it was a beautiful staircase, but I did not intend to stick around being miserable in Texas just so I could come down it one day in a long white dress. Besides, at the rate I was moving in meeting boys, let alone dating them, I would be at least fifty before I had any chance of getting married.

As usual, the air conditioner was humming away noisily so my parents did not hear me come in. I could hear their voices from the kitchen. I was about to announce my arrival when I froze in the hall. They were having an argument. In California they had fought about as much as the average parents fight, usually over stupid things like who left the top off the toothpaste and who overspent on the charge account. But I had noticed that the fights were becoming more frequent these days. My mother told me that my father was finding his new job very tough. My father is an easygoing person. He does not like a lot of hassles. He would be quite happy to be left alone with a glass of beer and a good book or a ball game on TV. In California he had been working for a small family outfit where everybody was close, but now he had moved to a big, highly competitive company. The pay was very good, and the prospects were good, too, but the strain was getting to him. My mother and I were getting used to having our heads snapped off when he came home. He usually snapped about stupid little things like leaving the sprinkler on too long or my forgetting to put away my bike. But tonight he was coming right to the nitty-gritty.

"Don't tell me you like it here any more than I do," he was shouting.

"Of course I miss California," I heard my mother answer calmly. She usually stayed calm. "But it won't be forever. We'll know if she's going to make the Olympics by next year."

"I can't see that we've helped her at all by bringing her out here. She doesn't seem happy to me." (I told you my father was the kindhearted one.)

"It's not a question of being happy," said my mother. "We had to let her go on training with Tod. She's been aiming for a goal for so long, we couldn't let her down now that she's almost reached it. It means more to her than anything in the world."

"To her or to you? Sometimes I don't think it would matter two hoots to her if she had to give up swimming completely."

"How can you say such a thing? She has dedicated her life to it."

"No. You have dedicated her life to it."

"Are you trying to say I've pushed her into something she didn't want to do?"

"All I'm saying is that I think we've gone too far with this move to Texas. We were all happier in California. And it's no good telling me I've got a better job here. It depends on how you rate better. But I'll tell you one thing, Moira. If I hadn't been the one driving that car that spoiled your chance to go to the Olympics, I'd have put my foot down long ago. As it is, you've managed to make me feel guilty."

I couldn't bear to stay and listen any longer. I was hearing things I had never heard before. Things I had only suspected, like nagging nightmares at the back of my mind. I think it comes as a shock to kids of my age to find out that their parents feel guilt and anger and frustration just like they do. Above all, I felt my own guilt—that I was the one who had been the cause of all this, that I had opened this can of worms.

I crept out the front door again and stood for a few moments breathing in the sweet, damp, decaying smell of the Texas evening. The frogs were croaking noisily, trying to outdo the cicadas. The whole scene sounded like sound effects from an old jungle movie. I felt very alone.

Then I took a deep breath and flung open the front door, slammed it behind me, and stomped noisily across the marble.

"Hi, everybody, I'm home!" I called. "What's for supper? I'm starving." Actually I was feeling desperately sick.

Chapter 4

Have you ever noticed that when you get a new car, every car you pass on the street seems to be the same make as yours? It was like that when my father bought our new Volkswagen Rabbit. I kept seeing all these other Rabbits everywhere we went.

Anyway, it was the same with Mark Waverly. I had been at Oak Creek for two months and had never seen him before, and now he was the first person I bumped into as I rushed in, late as usual, through the double doors the next morning. Actually I didn't really bump into him and knock his crutches flying. I just rushed past him.

"Hi," I said, by way of witty conversation.

The way he said hi back made me wonder whether he had already forgotten who I was. Not that I wasn't used to people forgetting who I was when I wasn't wearing a swimsuit, but I had been thinking a lot about Mark last night, and I suppose I assumed that he had been thinking about me, too.

In fact, I had done a lot of thinking last night. After a large helping of lasagna, which just would not slip down and which had to be scraped quickly into the garbage can when no one was looking, I pretended to be tired and went straight to bed. But I couldn't sleep no matter how hard I tried. I kept thinking about my parents' quarrel. They had never told me that we were moving to Texas because my coach was moving here. They had made it seem like it had been good luck that my father had landed this new job just in time for me to follow Tod. But now I knew that everything I suspected was true. They had only come here because of me. My mother didn't like it here, and my father hated his job, and they both expected me to make the Olympic team. The worst thing was that the way I was swimming right now I'd have a tough time making the qualifying time for the Nationals.

The more I thought about it the worse I felt. I could just imagine my mother next summer after I had blown my chance at the Nationals. "After all we have done for you—moving away from home, your daddy giving up his job and taking a new one he hates—and you let us down!"

I got out of bed and opened the French windows onto my balcony. Outside the night was soft and warm. The moon was floating upside down in the swimming pool. The frogs and insects were still croaking and chirping like an exotic jungle scene. It was a perfect late-summer night, the kind of night when you want to run barefoot through the grass. But of course in

Texas you didn't run barefoot anywhere because you might meet a snake.

When I shut the door again, I had made a decision. "I'll give myself a time limit. If I don't do well at spring Nationals, I'll quit."

I had never let myself think thoughts like that before. I had believed everything my mother and my coach had told me. I had believed that I could be the best flyer in the world.

"What will you do if you quit?" a nasty little voice nagged inside my head. "You'll just be a nothing. No good at anything. No friends. No ambitions—"

To stop these depressing thoughts, I switched my brain over to Mark Waverly. I imagined meeting him again, admiring his drawings, then making friends with him, being the one to bring him out of his depression.

That's why it came as such a shock when he hardly looked at me in the hall and said hi just as you'd say it to the clerk in the supermarket.

All morning I went through different emotions about him. First, I felt hurt that he didn't notice me, then I was angry that he could have forgotten me so quickly after drawing that beautiful picture of me.

By fourth period I had calmed down a bit and let reason take over. In fact, I had more or less convinced myself that he hadn't noticed me because he had this big test first period today and his mind was so fully on it that he wouldn't have noticed a Martian or Miss Universe.

So when I saw him in the cafeteria at lunchtime and noticed several spare seats near him, I took a deep breath and dared to sit down beside him.

"Oh, hi," I said, trying to sound casual but probably sounding phony. "You weren't saving these seats for someone, were you?"

He didn't smile, and he looked at me with those deep dark eyes. "People don't exactly flock to sit next to me anymore," he said. "But then they don't exactly seem to be hanging around you, either, do they?"

"I'm new here," I said. "I don't know anybody."

"You should do what the counselors tell you. Join some clubs. Why don't you join some clubs?" he asked. "They say that's a good way to meet people. They have all sorts of things going on after school."

"I don't have any time," I said. "I have swim practice every night after school."

"Oh, do you?" he asked, and I saw a flicker of interest in his dark eyes for the first time. "Where do you swim?"

"At the new swim center."

"Do they have a team there?"

"Yes, they're called the South Texas Marlins. They started only last year, I think."

"How come you don't swim on the high-school team?"

How could I say that my coach didn't think the high-school team would be good enough for me and he didn't want me to waste my precious practice time or wear myself out swimming in useless meets. Instead, I said, "I might next year. But this year I didn't get here in time for tryouts." I gave myself top marks for that lie.

I got the feeling he thought I had tried out for the high-school team and had not made it, because he looked almost kind. "It's pretty tough to get on a team at a big school like this," he said. "The competition, I mean. I remember when I—" He stopped suddenly, and his face became hard again. I guessed what he had been going to say: "I remember when I tried out for football."

We ate in silence for a while. He just picked at a bag of potato chips. I ate my pile of sandwiches. He noticed.

"How come you eat so much?" he asked.

"I get hungry."

"Don't you worry about getting fat? I thought all girls worried about getting fat."

"I swim five hours a day. That burns up a lot of calories."

"Five hours a day? Boy, you must be pretty serious about swimming."

I nodded and went on eating.

"You going to win the Olympics or something?" he asked. He sounded like he was making fun of me, and I blushed.

"You have to train hard if you want to be good at something," I said.

"Yeah, and sometimes you can waste your whole life training and it's all for nothing," he said bitterly. "Did you ever think of that?"

Then he looked at me hard as if he were seeing me for the first time.

"I don't even know your name," he said.

"It's Jennie. Jennie Webster."

"I'm Mark Waverly," he said. "But you needn't bother to remember that, because as soon as you've made some friends here, you'll forget I exist."

"Why should I do that? Aren't you being a bit melodramatic?"

"People don't like to hang around with cripples."

"That's dumb," I said.

"Maybe dumb, but it's true," he said.

"You're not even a cripple," I said. "Just because you are on crutches for a while doesn't make you a cripple."

"They think of me as a cripple," he said, "and that's what matters."

I didn't like the way the conversation was going, so I changed the subject quickly to what I thought was much safer ground.

"Have you been studying art long? You draw very well."

"I never took any lessons. It's just something I can do," he answered sharply.

I didn't take the warning and plunged straight on. "That picture of me was great. It looked just like me. Do you have more drawings with you? I'd really like to see some."

"I don't show my pictures to people," he said coldly. "They're private."

"Oh," I said. I felt as if I'd had my face slapped. But perhaps I was coming on rather strong. After all, I wasn't usually the sort of girl who started conversations with strange boys.

Perhaps I didn't know the right things to say or the right way to say them.

In embarrassed silence I gathered the remains of my lunch together. But I couldn't resist asking one last question. After all, out of all the people in the cafeteria yesterday, he had chosen me to draw.

"Mark, why did you do that drawing of me yesterday?"

I don't know what answer I expected to hear, but I know what I wanted to hear—that he'd thought I was pretty or interesting or mysterious . . .

"You want to know why?" he said. "Because you looked so damn depressed. You looked just like I feel."

I think I could have cried as I went out of the cafeteria. Now I understood what Marilyn had meant. Mark Waverly didn't seem to want friends. If I had been feeling sorry for myself before, I thought, it was nothing compared to Mark. Next to him, what did I have to complain about?

Chapter 5

My effort at curing Mark Waverly of his depression had failed. I admitted that fully. I felt so embarrassed about the whole thing that my face went as red as a radish whenever I thought about it. I decided then and there that I would never, ever, as long as I lived, make a fool of myself by talking to a strange boy again.

"Let's face it, Jennie Webster," I said, looking at myself in my bedroom mirror. "You are just not the type that boys go for. Golden Girls can walk up to strange boys and start talking, but you come on like a big phony when you try. You had better resign yourself to the fact that you will never come down those stairs in that long white dress, let alone be invited to homecoming."

I had found out all about homecoming the day before from Marilyn. She had come over to our house around nine o'clock to borrow a math book. As well as being boy crazy and a gossip, Marilyn was a champion borrower. She borrowed my shampoo at swimming, she borrowed my notes from the same classes she had attended. If we had been anything like the same size, I'm pretty sure she would have wanted to borrow my clothes.

Anyway, my mother let her into the front hall and did not look too pleased about it. I was up in my room, already getting undressed, and I peeked out to see who it was. My mother's voice floated up to me. "Oh, Marilyn, it's you." My mother made it quite clear that she did not like Marilyn. But Marilyn was either too thick-skinned or too dumb to notice.

"Isn't it rather late to be doing homework?" my mother asked frostily. "Jennie is getting ready for bed."

"Oh, I never do my homework before nine," Marilyn said, smirking. "And I never go to bed before eleven, at the earliest. That's when all the good TV shows finish."

"Well, I suppose you had better go up to Jennie's room and get the book you need," my mother said. "But please don't stay too long. Jennie has to be up for early practice."

Marilyn, I might add, could not be persuaded to come to early practice with the rest of the seniors. "I will do a lot of things to be near all those cute boys," she said. "But I will not get up at five in the morning for anyone."

So Marilyn breezed into my room, and I handed her the math book, feeling rather foolish in my shortie pajamas. She took the book and flipped through the pages, a look of disgust on her face. "I don't suppose you have the answers to this that I could borrow, do you?" she asked hopefully. "I just hate algebra. I can't seem to get the hang of it."

"I'm not showing you my answers, Marilyn," I said. "I'm not that great at it, either, so it wouldn't be any use copying from me."

She took this, as she took most things, with good nature.

"OK," she said. "I'll give the book back to you in the morning on the bus." Then she looked at herself quickly in my mirror, flipped back her hair with my brush, and turned to me. "Who's taking you to homecoming?"

"Homecoming? I thought that was just a football game."

She looked at me in wide-eyed disbelief, as if I had just said the Alamo was only a church. "Boy, were you ever born in the Dark Ages." She sighed. "Homecoming is only the biggest thing in the entire school year. There's the parade in the afternoon and the crowning of the homecoming queen and the game in the evening and then the best part—the homecoming ball."

I thought for a moment that she meant a leather thing that you throw, but it turned out that she meant a very grand sort of dance.

"The dresses are real fancy," she said, looking all dreamy-eyed, "and the boys rent tuxedos. And then there are the corsages—the boy has to buy the girl a corsage, and it has to be real big and real expensive. The best ones cost a hundred dollars!"

"Wow, who would pay that kind of money just for flowers?" I asked. She looked at me again as if I were from another planet.

"Why, everybody does," she said. "It's tradition. The boys all know it's expected of them, and they all know they have to take the girl out to a fancy restaurant after the dance is over."

"So can anybody actually afford to go to this thing?" I asked sarcastically.

She looked horrified. "If you don't go to homecoming, you are nothing," she said. "You are one great big zero!"

"Who's taking you?" I asked, deciding that attack was the best form of defense. I was pretty sure that no boy would want to spend a hundred dollars on flowers for Marilyn.

"Oh, I can't make up my mind," she said airily. "It's between Rob or Peter. I can't decide which of them I like best. They are both so cute. Or maybe Charley—the big blond guy who wears denim overalls—do you know him?"

"Well, let me know which one you decide on," I said cheerfully.

"I will," she said, picking up the math book from my dresser. "Thanks for the math book. See ya." Then she breezed out as I hoped she would.

At school the next day everybody was talking about nothing but homecoming. It seemed like everybody was going. All the girls were talking about who was taking them and how much the boys would spend on corsages and where they would go to eat dinner afterward. I began to realize that Marilyn had not exaggerated.

From listening to other people's conversations, it would appear I was the only junior who had not been invited by somebody. Even though I thought football was the most boring game in the world and that homecoming queens were even more boring, I found myself wishing that I could go. In fact, I felt a lot like Cinderella. Only I didn't have a fairy godmother. If I had, I would have made her wave her magic wand and get me straight out of Texas and back to California.

It's a good thing nobody had invited me, I thought, because my mother and Tod would both have forbidden me to go. The North-South All-Star meet was coming up, and I was never allowed to be out late when I was training for a meet. Tod had recently given me a pep talk about this all-star meet. Apparently, from what he said, the whole of South Texas was relying on me to beat the North single-handed. Not a very cheerful thought.

Neither were my thoughts of Mark Waverly. I decided to stay clear of him forever. I knew I couldn't face him again without blushing like a stupid little fifth-grader. So when I saw him coming down the hall toward me, I fled into the girls' bathroom instead of going to my locker as I had planned. I waited inside the bathroom until I had given him plenty of time to get down the hall and turn the corner at the end. Then I came out again and hurried to my locker. And who should be standing next to it but Mark Waverly himself! Immediately I turned from a girl into the human radish again.

I was not going to risk saying hi again.

After all, it hadn't worked the last two times. So I tried to ignore Mark and open my locker quite casually. Of course, as I turned the key I remembered that I had stuffed a whole bunch of things into it the night before, when I was in a hurry to catch the school bus. I remembered this about half a second too late because it all came falling out and clattered onto the stone floor. Everybody walking down the hall turned to look back in my direction. The only good thing was that my cheeks were already so red that they couldn't get any redder. I bent down to scoop up the stuff.

"Here, let me help," said Mark. "I'm not too good at bending, but you pass them up to me, and I'll put them back in the locker."

It only took a few seconds to pick up the whole lot. As I handed up a protractor to him without looking, our hands brushed. I drew mine back as if I'd been shocked.

"Here," he said and helped me to my feet.

"Thank you," I said unsteadily. "I feel like a fool."

"You don't have to," he said. "Things like that happen to everybody. You ought to try seeing how you feel when you fall down and can't get up again. I did that a couple of times when I first got the crutches. Now that really does make you feel dumb." And he almost smiled. I smiled back.

"I'd better hurry, or I'll never get to math on time," I said, gathering a pile of books.

"Jennie," he said, and I turned back to him again. "I was waiting by your locker because I wanted to give you this." He handed me a piece of paper. It was the sketch of me. He looked down at his feet and went on, "I felt bad about yesterday. I was rude to you. I guess I don't like people feeling sorry for me and patting me on the head and telling me to snap out of it and get going again. I didn't want anyone to know about my drawing, either. The guys I used to play football with—well, they would think it was odd. So I got a little uptight. But then I realized afterward that you weren't being nice because you felt sorry for me—you just needed someone to talk to. I guess it's tough changing high schools like that and not knowing anybody. Anyway, I'm sorry. I'd like you to have the drawing."

"Thank you," I said in a shaky voice. Our eyes met for a moment. Then he smiled, and his eyes had warm creases at the corners. "You know, I wanted to be a coward and slip this into your locker without your knowing. But you know what? I couldn't open your locker. It was locked. I guess that's why they call them lockers."

As we were both laughing, a boy came up to us. He was wearing his black and gold letter-jacket. "Hey, Mark, old buddy," he said. "You want me to come and pick you up and take you to the game?"

"I'm not going," Mark said, and the smile disappeared from his eyes.

"Hey, wait a minute—what do you mean you're not going?" The boy sounded horrified.

"Just what I said, Carl. I'm not going to homecoming."

"But you can't not go. We're counting on you. You know how all the guys expect you to be there. We've been together since junior high, Mark. It wouldn't be the same without you."

I could see Mark struggling with two emotions. Part of him felt guilty about letting his teammates down in any way, the other part felt angry at being treated like a mascot, sitting there watching his friends play.

"Well, OK," he said at last. "I'll go to the game, but I'm not coming to the dance. You won't catch me sitting there like a stuffed animal."

Carl patted him on the back. "I understand, old buddy. But I can tell the guys that we'll see you at the game?"

"You'll see me at the game," Mark said.

"Great, I'll come by your house for you," said Carl. "See ya." And he left.

I started to go, too.

"You going to the game?" Mark asked me.

"I don't think so."

"What's the matter, don't you like football?"

"Not too much."

He smiled. "You better not say things like that at this school, or you'll be strung from the nearest tree."

"Well, I don't know too much about football, really," I said. "Maybe I should go to the game."

Of course I was hoping he'd ask me to go with him. But he only said, "Well, I might see you there if you decide to go."

And that would have been that if fate hadn't come along in the person of Luanne Chapman. Luanne was the head Golden Girl. Of course I knew who she was. She was the first person everyone had pointed out to me in school. "That's Luanne. She's the leader of the Golden Girls." And they spoke in the same hushed voice as if they were saying, "That's the queen of England over there."

Luanne drifted by, swinging her hips and looking like something out of a shampoo commercial. I expected her to walk right by, but she stopped and tossed back her long blond curls.

"Hi, Mark," she said in a low silky voice that also sounded right out of a commercial. "How are you? Haven't seen you around in quite a while."

"I'm just fine, Luanne," he said.

"Great," she said. "I've been meaning to call you to tell you that if you want a ride to homecoming, I'm sure we can squeeze you in with us."

"That won't be necessary, Luanne," he said smoothly. "I'm taking Jennie here to homecoming."

"Oh," she said. "Oh, I see." Her gaze turned to me, as if she'd noticed me for the first time. My cheeks had gone back to normal human color, but now they flamed up again. Her eyes were gray-blue and very cold. It was like being looked at by a snake.

"Well," she said at last, "have fun, y'all," and she walked away swinging her shampoo-commercial hair.

Mark took a deep breath as she left.

"Look, I'm sorry about that," he said. "But she was just making me mad. I should have asked you first. But I really would like you to come to homecoming with me. I don't feel like going to the dance afterward. But you should see a really good football game once in your life."

"I'd like to come," I said.

"I wish I could say that I'll come and pick you up," he said, "but I can't drive because of my leg. That's a bummer, isn't it? Having to be driven around like a little kid."

"Perhaps I can get my father to let me drive his car," I said without too much conviction.

"That would be great," he said. "I really don't like the idea of that car pool, with all those other guys."

Then the bell rang loudly to announce that anyone who was not in the classroom would be marked tardy. I was late for math, and I didn't care. A real, live boy had asked me to homecoming. Not just any boy, either. Tall, good-looking Mark Waverly had asked me. I knew he had only asked me to spite Luanne Chapman, but I didn't care. I think I skipped all the way to math class.

Chapter 6

That afternoon I couldn't help tapping my personal information source, Marilyn, for the whole story on Mark and Luanne. We were in the showers together, and, as usual, she was borrowing my shampoo.

"Hey, Marilyn—was there ever anything between Mark Waverly and Luanne Chapman?" I asked casually as I took the bottle back from her before she emptied it all over her head.

"Mark and Luanne?" she asked, looking surprised. "You mean you haven't heard about them yet? They only used to be the hottest twosome in school. They were going together right up to his accident."

She paused to rinse off the first lather of shampoo. "It was just terrible," she confided. "When they told her he'd never walk again, she just broke up with him and started going with Chuck Harrison instead. You know him, don't you? The tall back with the blond, curly hair. He's real cute. . . . Hey, can I have that shampoo back for a minute if you've finished with it?" She paused to work up a second lather.

"You know what I heard?" she whispered, although the showers were so noisy I doubt anyone could have heard us. "They said when she heard that Mark would never walk again, she said she was too young to be tied down to a cripple. She walked right out of that hospital and got into Chuck's car and drove off. And I think—I think that Mark learned to walk again just to spite her."

She rinsed out her hair. "And you know what else I think? I think now that he's doing so well she might just want him back."

Well, she's not getting him back, I thought.

There was the small matter of talking my parents into homecoming. As I had thought, my mother immediately went into, "But the all-star meet is coming up so soon and Tod tells me the South is absolutely counting on you for their points."

I was about to say that I couldn't care less about the South or the North, but again she got in first. She has a knack of knowing what I am thinking. "Frankly, dear," she said, "I know you don't care if the whole of South Texas is washed away in the next hurricane. But this will be one quality meet where you'll actually have some competition. The whole of the Longhorn squad from Austin will be there."

I turned to my father, appealing to his softhearted nature. "Daddy, I'll be the only kid in the whole school who doesn't go to the football game. You said you wanted me to make an effort to fit in at school. Well, I'm making the effort. Some kids have asked me to go with them (slight stretching of the truth), and they'll think I'm odd if I don't go."

"Well, I don't know, honey," said my father, watching my mother's face for any reaction. He never actually went against her. "After all, as your mother says, this all-star meet is pretty important."

"But, Daddy, I'm not asking to stay out all night at the dance. I just want to go to the football game, that's all. It's over by ten or so. Then I'll come straight home. I promise."

"Oh, well, in that case"—there was a lot of eye contact between my parents, plus a few raised eyebrows and nods—"I think that will be all right. After all, it's only fair that you should join in school activities."

"Oh, thank you, Daddy," I cried and flung my arms around his neck. I had been so successful that I went a step further. "And, Daddy—I have this big favor to ask—"

"Short of money for a new outfit, eh?" Why did parents always think that favors had to be about money?

"No, it's nothing like that. We'll all be wearing jackets because it's at night, and it will be cold. But, Daddy, what I really want is—I mean, could I take the car? I'll be very careful, and it's only a few blocks. Everyone else will be going on to the dance afterward, so there won't be anyone to give me a ride home—"

But my father was already shaking his head. "You know how I feel about your driving here, Jennie. I know you are a good driver, but it's those other crazy fools, screeching along in pick-up trucks at ninety. And the teenagers are the worst. When I imagine how they'll be driving out of that football stadium, some of them full of beer too. . . . There is no way that you are going to have the car."

"How are all your friends getting to the game?" asked my mother. "Can't you go with them?"

"I told you, they are all going on to the dance. And besides, last time Daddy said he didn't want me driving with a bunch of kids."

"Quite right, I don't. I'll drive you there and pick you up afterward."

"Thank you, Daddy, that will be fine. By the way (I tried to be casual), could we give this friend of mine a ride, too?"

"Sure, where does she live?"

"It's a he."

"Oh," said my mother and father together.

"Won't he be going in his own car?" asked my mother suspiciously.

"He doesn't drive right now."

"Now that's something I thought didn't exist in the world anymore," said my father, laughing. "A teenager who doesn't drive."

"He had an accident last year, and he is still on crutches."

That turned out to be the best thing I could have told them. After all, not much harm could come to me with a guy on crutches.

It turned out that Mark lived very close to me. Outside of our new subdivision was a forest. It was a swampy South Texas forest of pine trees and magnolias and thick, choking undergrowth. Beyond the forest were farms. The first farm was Mark's. I don't know why, but I had sort of classed him as a humble farmboy. It wasn't because of the way he spoke. He had a trace of Texas in his speech, but he didn't say "ain't" and "y'all" the way a lot of the other kids did. Maybe it was because I was told that he lived on a farm and that, to me, meant humble country folk.

I got a shock when we went to pick him up on homecoming night. We turned into a long, white-fenced driveway, at the end of which was an enormous house looking more like *Gone with the Wind* than ours. It turned out that his father bred racehorses.

I had told Mark that my father would drive us, and it didn't seem to matter to him. When I introduced them, they shook hands and seemed to like each other. On the way to school, my father asked him about horses.

"That was the one good thing about my football accident," Mark said. "I probably won't be able to ride again, so I won't have to take over the stables. My father had always made it very clear that he expected me someday to take over the ranch. I was always wondering how I could get out of it. You see, I never did like horses much. To tell you the truth, they scare me a bit, and they always know when someone is scared of them. What I wanted to do was get a football scholarship and then maybe play pro ball. Now I don't know what I'll do."

The Oak Creek stadium was ablaze with lights and packed with excited kids. (And looking around the crowd I could see there were quite a few excited moms and dads, too.) We had great seats right at the front of the bleachers, saved especially for Mark. The bleachers were so full that we had to sit really close to each other. I didn't mind.

I didn't think that I could feel in any way excited about a football game, but in the last moments before the band came out, I found I was as excited as anyone. Then, with a tremendous clash of cymbals and fanfare of trumpets, the band burst out, playing the theme from *Rocky*. Out into the spotlight they came—two never-ending lines of black and gold. Out ran the Golden Girls, the lights sparkling on their golden sequins. Suddenly I found I had a lump in my throat, and I wondered when I had felt like this before. Then I remembered. It was the first time I made it to the Far Western Championships. Before the meet started, they raised the flag and played the national anthem. I remember feeling, this is *it*! It's really happening to me. The big time! I felt as important as if I had won the Olympics. Even when I climbed up the steps and stood on the top one to get my medal for winning Junior Nationals, I didn't feel nearly as important as when they raised the flag when I was ten.

The band marched up and down, forming different patterns. The Golden Girls did some fantastic things with cartwheels and splits and finished with a big pyramid—naturally with

Luanne, looking more gorgeous than ever, perched on top. Then a great roar went up as the team ran out. As they ran past Mark, they each looked up at him and gave him a solemn wave. He waved back, looking cool and cheerful, but I, who was beside him, could sense his mixed emotions.

It was a terrific game. I don't remember much about the plays, but I know I did a lot of leaping up and down and screaming as loud as any Golden Girl when our team scored. Three minutes to the end the score was tied at fourteen. Then there was a fantastic pass. Chuck Harrison seemed to fly up into the air like Superman. Somehow, his hand curled around the ball, and he was running, running, defenders crumpling on both sides of him. The crowd, including me, was up and screaming as he flung himself to make the touchdown.

It was all over. We had won. Everybody in the stands was hugging everybody else. Mark sat and didn't hug anybody.

"Let's let these crazy people go first," he said, pulling me down beside him. So we sat and watched the stadium empty. Neither of us spoke. I wondered if he was remembering this game last year and if last year it had been he who made that winning touchdown. Then at last he got to his feet.

"What time did you tell your father to come?" he asked as we made our way out of the deserted stadium.

"Ten."

"It's only just after nine," he said. "How

about if we look in at the dance for a few minutes after all?"

"I thought you didn't want to go."

"I changed my mind."

"But I'm not dressed for a dance."

"Me neither. We'll just go down to say hi. OK?"

"Fine with me." Who but an idiot would refuse to go to a dance with Mark Waverly just because she was wearing old cords, running shoes, and a big blue parka?

We walked side by side across the campus. People hurried past us. Most of them recognized Mark and called out to him. I wondered how Mark was feeling. I knew that if I could never swim again, I would not have gone to watch someone else swimming. Was he feeling depressed now? I stole a glance at him. He looked back, and then he grinned.

"I thought you were supposed to be the girl who didn't like football," he said. "You were yelling louder than anyone. And you were jumping around so much I thought you'd fall out of the bleachers."

"I never thought I'd feel like that about football, either."

"Maybe we'll turn you into a Texan yet," he said.

Music was already spilling out of the gym as we came up the path. A car drew up, and a couple got out in full formal dress. He was wearing a dark-blue tux with a ruffled shirt, and she was in a long, flowing apricot-color dress, like a Greek goddess. On her shoulder was a huge spray of chrysanthemums. The ribbons had "Tina and Frank" embroidered on them in glitter. It was horrible and showy and must have cost a fortune. Still, I couldn't help feeling a tinge of envy that I was not that girl going to the dance in that beautiful dress with the proof of a boy's devotion flying from my shoulder for all the world to see.

As they passed us, Mark stopped short.

"I just remembered. I forgot something," he said. "Wait right there. Don't move. I'll be right back." Then he disappeared off across the front lawn as fast as his crutches would let him—which was pretty fast. I was left alone in the darkness with a million thoughts racing through my mind. Had he lost his nerve and decided to skip the dance? Didn't he want to be seen with me? I began to feel more and more insecure. Then there was the click of his crutches again along the path, and he appeared, looking very pleased with himself.

"No girl can go to the dance without a corsage," he said. "Here." And he handed me some large red flowers. They were beautiful, but they looked very familiar.

"Where on earth did you get these?" I asked suspiciously.

"Young ladies aren't supposed to ask their escorts where they got the corsage," he said. "Go ahead. Put them on."

Then I remembered where I had seen them. They were growing outside the principal's office, beside the front entrance to the school.

"I can't," I protested. I didn't want to be seen wearing stolen flowers.

"Here, I'll help you," Mark said, threading them through my buttonhole. He stepped back and looked at me. "Now I think we are suitably dressed to go to the dance." He led me inside.

I felt really embarrassed as we made our way in between all those handsome couples in their evening wear. But Mark didn't seem to mind, and the dancers all seemed happy to see him. In no time at all we were at a table with Cokes.

"You know," he said thoughtfully, playing with the straw of his Coke, "I thought it would be much worse to come and watch the other guys play tonight instead of me. I didn't think I could do it. But it wasn't so bad."

"I think you were very brave to come."

"I had one bad moment. Just when they played the national anthem at the beginning. I nearly walked out then. I kept saying to myself, 'That won't ever be you again out there.' "

"How do you know you won't ever play football again?" I asked, feeling suddenly brave. "They said you might not walk again, and you're walking pretty well. I'm sure if you exercise that bad leg it will be as good as new."

"What do you know about it?" Mark asked so fiercely that I almost fell off my chair. "This leg is useless, I tell you. I can't even feel it. It will never be any use again."

"I'm sorry," I said. "It was none of my business."

"No, I'm sorry," he said. "I have a bad temper. That was my Irish grandmother's fault. I explode before I can stop myself. I guess that was what made me a good football player." Then he touched my hand. "Hey, I really want to thank you for coming with me tonight. I don't think I would have gone through with it if I'd been on my own."

"I had a great time," I said.

"It's good that we're such near neighbors," Mark said. "Maybe you can come over some day after school."

"If I ever have time between swim practice and homework."

"Oh, yeah. I'd forgotten swim practice. Hey—you know what? I'd like to see you swim sometime. Can I come and watch?"

"You mean watch me practice?"

"Sure. I never saw a swim team before. Can I come?"

"If you want to. Only I warn you, it's pretty boring. We just go up and down hundreds of times."

"No, I'd really like to come. Honestly."

"OK. How about next week? That's my mother's car pool week, so it would be easy to pick you up."

"OK," he said, smiling. "I'd like to take a look at the future Olympic champion."

Then the music got too loud for talking, and we just sat and watched the dancers. At least Mark was watching the dancers, including Luanne, who was swinging her hips in a skin-tight, royal-blue dress. I hardly noticed any of them because I had just seen something very interesting. I looked several times just to make sure—but I had not been wrong.

So much for you and your bad leg, Mark Waverly, I thought. *You're just a phony. I'm going to find a way to make you give up those crutches if it's the last thing I do.*

I had been looking at Mark's feet. They were tapping in time to the music. Both of them.

Chapter 7

I thought a lot about Mark and his leg over the next few days. He claimed that he had no feeling in his left leg—and yet I had seen him moving his foot to the music. It didn't make sense. Why would a strong, athletic boy like Mark pretend that his injury was worse than it really was?

I saw Mark almost every day. We often had lunch together, and he seemed to enjoy my company. He even told me he'd like to show me his drawings, which I thought was great progress. But I was realistic enough to know that I was not "Mark's girl." He was grateful to have someone to talk to who had not known him before the accident. I don't think he even noticed I was a girl. I have that effect on boys. All the boys from my California car pool used to be great buddies and laugh and tease me, but, as one of them said, "You're just like one of the guys, Jennie!" No one would ever have said that to Luanne Chapman.

Right now it was useful to be like one of the guys because it put no pressure on Mark. He could talk to me because I was a newcomer and a stranger. Some days he was bad-tempered and moody, some days he was cheerful. Some days he even talked about football and some of the things he had done. But never about the future. Never, "When I get back on my feet again . . ."

Slowly I began to understand why he didn't want to give up those crutches. He was afraid. He might be a big, hulking six foot two, but he was still afraid. He had always been a superstar, an outstanding athlete ever since he went to school. When he walked around on crutches, people remembered that he had been the star. If he recovered but couldn't play again, he'd be a nobody. I understood just how he felt because I had the same feelings myself. I was frightened of being a nobody if I quit swimming. But I couldn't talk to Mark about it. Not yet.

Mark came to watch me swim on Tuesday night. My mother was very suspicious of a strange boy coming to interrupt my training, but when she actually met Mark and he said, "Yes, ma'am," in that smooth, deep voice of his, I could see that she thought he was OK. As for Lori from the car pool, she could not keep her eyes off him all the way to the swim center. She flirted and told him that boys always thought she was very mature for her age. I was surprised at the wild surge of jealousy I felt as she fluttered her eyelashes at him. I need not have worried, though. He gave me a quick look that said he found her just as stupid as I did.

Tod was setting up the time clock as I brought Mark out to the deck. He immediately jumped to the conclusion that I was bringing new talent to the team. Since coming to Texas and having only about forty swimmers to work with, Tod had acted like a Hollywood talent scout to anyone vaguely hopeful for the team.

"Glad to meet you," he said, pumping Mark's hand. "What happened to your leg?"

"Football injury," Mark said.

"That's tough," Tod said. "You ought to come and swim. Nothing like swimming for building up the muscles again."

"It wouldn't be much use," Mark said stiffly. "I've damaged the nerves in my left leg."

"Swimming helps anything," said Tod. "I'll guarantee you full use of that leg again. Come and try it sometime. I'll show you exercises to do. And go watch Jennie work out on the universal gym. That's great for strengthening weak muscles, too."

I thought Mark might get angry again, so I said quickly, "Yeah, come and watch my torture session," and we left.

I swam well that day—one of the few times I had swum well since leaving California. Of course I wanted Mark to see me at my best, so I did every set flat out, and Tod didn't have to yell at me once. In fact, as I got out of the pool, Tod came and put an arm around me.

"Is that the boyfriend?" he asked, nodding at Mark.

"He's just a friend," I said.

Tod grinned. "Well, tell him to come every day," he said. "You haven't worked like that since you wanted to beat Ricky."

I flung a towel over my shoulders, took off my cap, and walked over to Mark, who was sitting alone in the empty bleachers.

"Did you get bored?" I asked him. "Workouts aren't very exciting to watch."

He looked at me very strangely as he stood up. "I had no idea," he said.

"About what?"

"About you. When I teased you at school about being an Olympic champion, I really didn't think—I mean—to see you at school you don't even look like an athlete. But the way you move through the water—especially when you do the butterfly— you're good!"

"Thanks!" I said.

Tod had come up behind me and overheard. "Yes," he said, "she's not bad—when she works." And he gave me a wink as he walked away.

Chapter 8

Winter comes suddenly to Texas. There is no such thing as fall—a nice, leisurely turning yellow of the leaves with warm days and cool nights. In South Texas it stays hot right until a cold front comes through from the north. It turned cold right after the day Mark came to watch me swim. When I got to morning workout, I found the temperature was 35 degrees and the pool heater wasn't working.

"I can't swim in this," I told Tod.

"It will be fine by tomorrow," he reassured me. "Just get in and work harder than usual."

But it was no use. Being a skinny person, I feel the cold very easily. Between sets my teeth chattered so much that Tod thought I was putting it on.

"Quit fooling around, Jennie, it isn't that cold," he snapped.

But it was that cold. At the end of practice I threw up. And I dreaded afternoon workout.

"It will be better by tomorrow. I've talked to the maintenance man again, and they're going to turn up the heater," Tod promised. But it wasn't. It was worse because the pool heater still wasn't working and the water had cooled even more.

To make things worse, it was raining—a stinging, icy rain that bounced off our backs as we swam. Tod stood huddled under a big umbrella, and even he had to admit that we couldn't go on working in these conditions.

I could not have felt more depressed if I tried. The all-star meet was only a few days away, and how was I expected to practice when I could hardly move my arms in the freezing water? Worse still, Mark would never come and sit in the freezing rain to watch me again. He probably wouldn't even come until spring. I'd never persuade him to try to swim and get that leg moving again.

You have a long time to think when you are swimming a thousand-yard warm-up, and these were the sort of miserable thoughts that kept going through my mind.

The morning workout set the mood for the whole day. When I didn't even meet Mark in the cafeteria, I told myself that he was avoiding me. I was sitting alone in the cafeteria, brooding over a tuna fish sandwich (and that was another bad thing about the day—I hate tuna, and my mother had bought a whole lot of cans on special), when I heard a cheerful "Hi, y'all" behind me. I turned around, and it was Marilyn, wearing a bright-red blouse and tight white jeans. "You alone?" she asked.

I nodded.

She sat down beside me without waiting to be asked and took out a stick of celery. Marilyn was on a constant diet, but it never seemed to do any good. "Well, how come you're looking sour enough to curdle milk?" she asked.

I didn't want to tell her that I was upset about Mark. I knew anything I told Marilyn would be all over school in two seconds flat.

"I'm fed up with swimming in cold water," I said, and it was true. "I feel like I'm going to catch double pneumonia."

"I don't know why you do it," Marilyn said. "You won't catch me coming near that pool again until they heat it properly. First, I do not wish to freeze to death and second, it is impossible to look sexy when your skin is blue."

I smiled in spite of myself. Marilyn might be a hopeless gossip, but it was hard not to like her, in a way that you might like a big, bouncy pet dog. She never stopped being friendly, whatever happened. And sometimes a friend is a good thing to have around.

"I have no choice," I said. "I have to go on swimming, heater or no heater. I only have a few months until Nationals, and if I don't do well, my mother will tear me limb from limb."

"Yeah, that mother of yours." Marilyn sighed. "She's worse than mine, and that's saying a lot. Why don't you tell her to get off your back? Tell her you're going to quit."

"But I don't want to quit," I said.

"Well, in that case, you need your head examined," Marilyn said. "What you really need," she added, giving me a knowing look, "is a cute boy to take your mind off all this swimming. It's not healthy for a girl of your age to think about swimming all the time. There are better things in the world, you know. How about that Mark Waverly?" she suddenly demanded. "I see you eating lunch with him most days. And he took you to homecoming—and he even came to watch you at swim practice, didn't he?"

How did she manage to know every detail of my private life? I played with my sandwich and said nothing.

"Well," she demanded loudly, "are you two going together or aren't you?"

Several heads turned toward us.

"He's just a friend, that's all," I muttered, tearing apart my sandwich.

"That's what they always say in the movie magazines, right before they elope to Las Vegas," Marilyn said.

"Look, Marilyn," I pleaded, "Mark doesn't even notice I'm a girl."

She looked horrified. "Then make him notice. Wear sexy clothes, like I do."

I tried not to smile at the thought of me in Marilyn's clothes. Marilyn had finished her stick of celery. "I have to get moving," she said. "Tracy promised I could borrow her chemistry notes, and I have to study up for my history test. But I tell you one thing, Jennie. If I wanted a boy, I'd go right out and get him. See ya."

Then she was gone, and I was as gloomy as ever. Just how did you begin to go right out and get him? That was the question.

The afternoon was as bad as the morning. We had two tests, one in chemistry and one in social studies. In chemistry I realized that I didn't know the difference between carbon fourteen and carbon anything else. In social studies we had a test on Texas history. How was I supposed to know any more Texas history than the Alamo?

I almost decided to skip swim practice by claiming sickness. In fact, I did feel pretty terrible. I had a scratchy throat and throbbing head, but that could just be after struggling through two tests. But in the end, dedication (and the thought of a long argument with my mother) got the better of me, and I went.

"You guys—guess what?" one of the little kids greeted us. "We're going to swim in the indoor pool, isn't that great?"

It was great in theory. In theory, it was better than the stinging rain and the freezing water. In practice, it was much worse. The indoor pool was the teaching pool. It was designed to teach little kids to swim and therefore was kept around ninety degrees. The air we had to breathe was almost as hot. If you've ever tried swimming in your bathtub, you know how exhausting that is.

In addition, the diving team was also scheduled to work out at the same time, so we had to give up the entire deep end of the pool.

Tod crowded us all into three lanes, and I might as well have stayed home, because working out was impossible. I went first, of course, but I was soon lapping the slowest people in my lane or trying in vain to lap them and getting stuck behind them while they thrashed around and kicked me in the face.

Tod soon saw that we were all wasting our time and finished practice early. His decision might also have been helped by the fact that sweat was pouring down his face.

I took off my cap and shook out my hair in the water. Then I did a couple of back dives to try to liven my spirits. I was just about to get out when I saw a pair of feet beside the pool—feet with crutches beside them.

"Hi, mermaid," said Mark.

"What on earth are you doing here?"

"My little sister had to come for gymnastics class, so I thought I'd tag along and spy on you. I missed you at lunch today. I had this horrible chemistry test right before lunch, and I had to stay and finish it."

"We had a chemistry test, too. Right after lunch. Mr. Schiffman must have been in a bad mood today to hand out tests to everyone."

"How did you do?"

"Terrible. I had to guess at half the answers."

"Me, too."

He smiled down at me. "See, we have a lot in common after all. We are both bad at chemistry. Come on out of there—do you have time for a soda before your car pool comes?"

"If I hurry and miss my shower," I said. "Here—help me out."

I reached up a hand to him, and he grabbed it. Suddenly he lost his balance and fell forward into the water. He hit the surface with a huge splash. I swear I didn't pull him in. At least I don't think I did. At least I didn't do it on purpose. But I have to admit I was pleased it happened. I have my senior lifesaving certificate, so I could have coped if he had gotten into trouble, but he didn't. Spluttering, Mark came to the surface a few yards from the side. He shook the water out of his hair and eyes, then swam to the side and grabbed it.

"How the hell did that happen?" he asked, looking a bit scared and a bit angry.

"I guess you didn't have enough hands for one girl and two crutches," I said, trying not to smile. "But I'll tell you what—there was nothing wrong with your swimming. You kicked with both legs."

He looked surprised. "You're right. I think I did. Let's see." Cautiously, he swam a few strokes down the side of the pool. When he grabbed the side again, he looked very pleased.

"It's much better than I thought," he said. "I could make the leg move OK. Maybe I will come and work out like your coach said."

"Hey, that would be great."

Suddenly a wicked light came into his eyes. "I'll race you to the steps," he said suddenly. Immediately he started thrashing his way down the pool ahead of me. It was only a few yards to the steps, and of course he got there first.

"You see, I beat you," he yelled in glee. "My first swim and I beat the future Olympic champion."

We sat together laughing on the steps.

"You'd better get home and into some dry clothes before you catch pneumonia," I said at last. "And my mother will be here and wondering where I've gone."

"Get my crutches, will you?" he asked, coming back to reality with a bump.

"You might not need these much more," I said.

"Oh, it won't go as quickly as that," he said, and the confidence had gone from his face.

As we walked away from the pool, we met my mother hurrying in through the swinging doors. She stopped short when she saw us.

"What on earth?" she squeaked.

"Your daughter has been giving me a swimming lesson," said Mark.

My mother could only watch open-mouthed as we walked past her together.

Chapter 9

After falling fully clothed into the pool, it was Mark who should have caught a cold. Instead, my own scratchy throat turned into a full-fledged cold of the most streaming type. I knew the all-star meet was only a few days away, so I struggled bravely to swim practice. It was terrible. Have you ever tried swimming when you can't breathe? I would lift my body out of the water with each fly stroke, take a big breath, and gasp in no air at all.

In the end, even the slave-driving Tod had to admit I was sick.

"Go home and dose yourself up, for pete's sake. Drink lemon juice and honey. Rub stuff on your chest. Whatever it takes to get you well again. And you'd better not come to practice tomorrow."

Even though I felt terrible, I felt pleased at the same time. It wasn't often I got a day off from swimming—with my coach's blessing. And I knew what I was going to do with that day, too—I was going to ride my bicycle over to Mark's house and see his drawings.

"You mean you don't have to swim for a

whole day?" Mark teased me at lunchtime. "What will you do with yourself? Do you think you'll suffer from withdrawal symptoms?"

"Actually, I thought I might ride over to your house if you're not doing anything after school."

"Do you think I ever do anything these days?"

"I meant if you're going to be home."

"Do I ever go anywhere else?"

"Oh, stop feeling sorry for yourself, Mark Waverly. And you *do* go out and do things. How many other guys in this school fell in a swimming pool this week?"

He laughed and put an arm around my shoulder. "You're good for me, you know that?"

That arm felt strong and heavy on my shoulder. It felt good. It was like letting all the school know "this girl belongs to me." I didn't think for a moment that Mark really meant it that way. It was meant to be a "good friends" type of arm and nothing more. But my one semester of psychology told me that it still meant he felt possessive about me. As for the rest of the school—they could think what they liked.

"Will you show me the rest of your drawings tonight?" I asked as we walked down the hall together.

"I don't know about these fresh California girls," he said. "Didn't anyone ever tell you that it was the man who was supposed to invite the lady to his room to see his etchings? She's not meant to invite herself!"

"Well, if you don't want me to come—"

"Of course I want you to come—even though you do look pretty contagious to me. You'd better not get too close to me!"

People hurried past us. "Hi, Mark. Hi, Jennie," they said. They actually knew my name now. That was one of the good things about being with Mark. Everybody knew him, and if everybody thought that I was Mark's girl, he didn't make them think otherwise. Neither did I.

I glanced at the bulletin boards as we walked along. Suddenly one of the notices caught my eye. I read it quickly and decided to come back and take down all the details.

"What are you looking at?" Mark asked, turning around to wait for me.

"Nothing. Just this lecture I might want to go to."

"You won't be allowed to miss swim practice," Mark teased as I caught up with him.

But it hadn't been a notice about a lecture.

That afternoon I rode over to Mark's house. I was really being a bit sneaky, I have to confess. My mother had to drive the car pool to swimming, and she usually did her shopping there rather than hang around the center for a couple of hours or use all that gas coming home again.

"Now, you're sure you'll be all right?" she asked, looking worried. "Stay warm, will you?"

"I'm fine, Mom. I just have a runny nose. That's all."

"Well, we don't want it to turn into flu before the meet, do we?"

"No, Mom." (I was playing the good daughter.)

Actually, I didn't like fooling my mother, but I knew exactly what she would say if I told her I wanted to go to Mark's. She would say, "If you're not well enough to swim, you are not well enough to leave the house." Something like that. And probably a lot about, "We hardly know the boy. We don't know if he's a suitable friend for you," etc., etc., etc.

In this case, I knew he was a suitable friend, and I also knew that a ten-minute bicycle ride would not hurt me. So I went.

"Have you come to see my etchings?" asked Mark, giving me a mock leer as he opened the front door.

Before I could answer, another door opened and a pint-sized girl, dark and large-eyed like Mark, stuck her head out.

"Hi," she said. "I'm Josie. I know all about you."

"Get lost, Josie," said Mark.

"It's good manners to introduce a stranger to your sister," she said, wrinkling her nose at him.

"You said you knew all about her, so you don't need to be introduced. Now get lost, will you."

"OK, OK, I'm going," she said. But she didn't.

"Come on. Let's go to my room," said Mark, frowning at her.

"Ooohee—Mark's got a girl in his room," Josie sang out. Then she ducked and ran as

Mark threw a magazine from the hall table at her.

"She's the pits," he said, opening a door for me. "You're lucky not to have any kid sisters or brothers."

"I don't know," I said. "If I had about five brothers or sisters, my parents wouldn't be able to spend so much energy worrying about me."

"But they wouldn't be able to afford for you to swim, either."

"Sometimes I wonder if that would be such a bad thing."

"Don't you like swimming?"

"I suppose I do, or I'd probably quit. But you know, I've spent most of my life working out every day. I really can't imagine what it would be like having nothing to do in the evenings."

"I know just what you mean. I had football practice and games all fall and baseball all summer—and then suddenly I had all this free time. Free time isn't all it's cracked up to be. You can get really tired of TV."

"You have your drawings. Are you going to show them to me?"

"Sure, I'll get them out. Would you like me to get you a Coke first?"

"No, thanks. I can't taste anything with this cold, anyway."

"Yeah—you look pretty terrible."

"Thanks. You really know how to flatter a girl."

"I didn't mean it like that, and you know it. You look fine. Your cold looks pretty terrible. I better watch out that you don't come too close to me."

But for a second he was close to me. I was very conscious of him looking down at me, smiling. Then he seemed to think better of it and moved away. "I'll find you those drawings," he muttered.

He went to the closet and opened it. While he was looking inside, I had time to look around his room. Nice, matching oak furniture with a built-in desk and bookshelves. Everything in its proper place and all very tidy.

Either he has a fantastic mother or he's naturally tidy, I thought in amazement, not being naturally tidy myself. The closet was tidy, too. He brought out a big box and opened it. It was full of all sorts of drawings. He took out some and spread them over the floor.

"These are some of the more recent ones," he said.

I could find nothing to say. The sketch of me had been good, but some of these were fantastic. Drawings of sleek racehorses and soft foals, landscapes and ranches, trees and dogs, and people's faces.

"Mark, these are great," I managed to say at last. "What does the art teacher at school say about them?"

"I've never shown them to him," he said. "In fact, I've never shown them to anyone—except you."

"But why? You're so talented. It's wrong not to use that talent."

"I couldn't show them to anyone at school.

You don't understand. I was the big football jock. If I show them my pictures, they'll all say, 'Poor old Mark—used to be so tough and now all he can do is draw little pictures.' "

I had been going to tell him about the notice on the board at school. It had been for an art contest among all Texas high-school kids for drawings on a Texas theme. The first prize was an art scholarship and your picture exhibited in the state capitol building in Austin.

"Did you ever think of making a career in art?" I asked.

He laughed. "What kind of career would that be? I've only wanted to do one thing with my life and that's be a pro football player. Now I don't want anything."

I decided not to mention the competition after all. Instead, I asked, "When are you going to start coming to swim in the afternoons? My coach said you could use the indoor pool anytime. If you come during swim-team hours, he'll give you some exercises to work on."

"I'll think about it," Mark said. "I just have to convince myself that it's not all for nothing. I practiced football every day for years, and it was all for nothing. I don't want to spend my time in a pool and then find my leg won't get any better."

"But it's got to. All you need is to build up some strength—"

"The doctor said the nerves are permanently damaged, and I shouldn't hope for too much. Do you think you know more than he does?" Mark snapped.

"OK. Forget it," I said. "I think I'd like that Coke after all if you're still offering."

"Sure," he said, and went out.

As soon as he left, I acted quickly. I had made a decision while we were arguing. Something had to happen to get Mark's self-confidence back. I was sure he could do well in the art contest. I was also sure that he would never enter it. So I snatched up one of the pictures. It was a drawing of Mark's ranch with the white picket fence, two beautiful horses, and the barn in the distance. I slipped it inside my jacket, which lay on the bed. Now all I had to do was hope he didn't miss it. But there were so many similar pictures that I didn't think that was too likely.

He came back with the Coke as I was gathering up the pictures and trying to look relaxed and cool.

"These are really good, Mark," I said. "If I were you, I'd show them to everybody."

He grunted but didn't answer.

"I better be getting back, or my mother will catch me out," I said, carefully lifting my jacket from the bed. "Thank you for showing them to me, and thank you for the Coke."

"See you tomorrow," he said. "Take care of that cold."

"I will."

"By the way," he said as I was about to open the door, "can I come and watch your swim meet on Sunday?"

"Sure. It's down in Houston, and we leave before seven in the morning, but you can come if you want to."

"I want to see the future Olympic champion in action," he said, grinning.

"The way the future Olympic champion feels at the moment, you might witness a drowning whale."

"Don't worry. I'll dive in and save you."

Right on cue Josie appeared again, sniggering stupidly. "You going already?" she asked innocently.

"I have to be home before it gets dark."

"Too bad Mark can't drive anymore," she said. "His TransAm is just sitting there in the garage. Mom wants to sell it."

"Nobody's selling my TransAm," Mark said fiercely.

"OK. Fight with Mom, not me," Josie said.

"I really have to go now, Mark," I interrupted awkwardly. Being an only child, I wasn't used to family arguments. They always embarrassed me.

Mark opened the front door for me, and I walked down the steps.

"See ya," he said, waving.

As I got on my bike I heard Josie speaking loudly. I was sure she meant me to hear her. "How come you like her? She's not nearly as pretty as Luanne."

I didn't hear Mark's answer.

Chapter 10

The day of the all-star meet arrived, and I wasn't feeling much better. It was true that my nose was no longer running, but my chest now felt as if I were breathing through a sieve. And I had a cough.

I didn't say much as my mother drove us down to Houston. It was still dark and very cold. Our breath in the car was like dragon's breath for the first few miles, and I coughed a lot. As we neared the city, the first pale streaks of dawn were showing, and the skyscrapers were outlined against the pink glow.

My mother was always the one to drive to meets. My father never did. He said he got too nervous for me and it was better for us all if he stayed home. Secretly I think he enjoyed sleeping in and having a late breakfast with no interruptions.

My mother had not minded Mark coming with us, but she was no great talker in the morning. In fact, she always drove with a coffee cup clutched in one hand, taking sips every now and then. She never really came alive until she had drunk several cups of strong black coffee.

Mark sat hunched behind me, his long legs curled into the back-seat space, and said cheerful things every now and then. I answered in grunts. Actually, I always feel so nervous before a meet that I find it hard to speak. My stomach feels as if a cold iron hand is clutching at it—and I always think about going to the bathroom!

I caused quite a stir as I changed in the locker room. As a newcomer to Texas, not many of these girls had seen me before. Only the ones who were at the Junior Nationals. They whispered to the others, and I found faces peeping between lockers to take a look at me. I wanted to giggle. I wished I had invented some routine, like meditating or standing on my head, to give them something to look at.

During warm-up my arms felt like lead. I pulled as hard as I could on each stroke, but I didn't seem to be going anywhere.

"I really don't feel like swimming in this meet," I told Tod as I climbed out of the pool. "Do I have to?"

"Of course you have to. It's your first meet in Texas. Everybody wants to see you swim."

"If they see the way I'm swimming today, they'll all laugh!"

"Come on, Jennie. Be realistic," Tod said. "Even if you are off your best times, don't worry too much. There aren't too many national-class swimmers in the meet. It should be a piece of cake."

Let me tell you I was not looking forward to this piece of cake at all. After warm-up I felt all shivery and came over to sit next to Mark. He was busy reading the program and looked up to take the doughnut I was offering him.

"Do you know that you are the top seed in this meet?" he asked, his surprise showing on his face. "Look at this: One hundred butterfly, J. Webster. Two hundred individual medley, J. Webster. One hundred freestyle, J. Webster.' "

I nodded and went on eating a chocolate doughnut. I had expected me to be the top seed. Obviously Mark hadn't.

"I knew you were a good swimmer," he said, "but I didn't realize you were that good. That must mean you are the best in Texas, right?"

"Best in Texas?" said my mother from the next seat. "She won the Junior Nationals last year!"

"So you're the best in the whole USA?"

"That was only Junior Nationals," I said. "Tod hasn't let me compete in Senior Nationals yet. Junior Nationals have a couple of seconds slower qualifying times, and it's like a practice meet for real Nationals."

"Where do you think you'd place in the Senior Nationals?"

I shrugged my shoulders and struggled between being modest and being realistic. "Somewhere in the top six," I said.

"Fantastic!" Mark said. "You really are a future Olympian." Looking serious, he took my hand and shook it. "Mighty proud to know you, ma'am," he said in a mock southern gentleman voice.

My first race was the North versus South relay. I was swimming the fly leg for the South. After the back and breast, we were way behind, and I thought that even I, swimming at my best, couldn't catch up for us. But luckily the North had put in a very weak flyer, and I was able to hand over about a three-yard lead. The freestyler just about managed to hold off the North girl, and we won.

"First gold medal of the day," said my mother, looking pleased. "One down, three to go."

"Mother, please," I begged, looking around in embarrassment. She was always saying things like that, and I was always wishing the floor would open up and swallow me.

"Well, judging by that relay, the North doesn't seem to have any swimmers who can give you a good race," my mother said.

"They might be saving their best for individual events," I answered.

"What do you mean?" Mark asked.

"In this meet you are only allowed to swim a total of four events. That can be three events plus a relay, like me, or four individual events with no relays, or two events and two relays. It's up to the coaches where they put their swimmers to get the most points."

My guess about saving their swimmers for individual events was right. In the hundred-yard freestyle I recognized the girl in the next lane. She came from Austin, and I had met her at the Junior Nationals.

"Hi, Caroline," I said.

"Hi," she said. "I didn't think you lived in Texas. Didn't you swim for Santa Barbara?"

"I used to. My coach moved here, and I moved with him."

"My bad luck. I took it for granted I'd be top seed in this meet. Then you came along." She grinned as she said it.

"Sorry. I'll go back to California if you like."

We both laughed and shook hands as we mounted the blocks. Swimming is nice like that. Most people you meet are really friendly even if they are your rivals. Once we were on the blocks, though, she became my rival again. I was aware of her black suit and orange cap out of the corner of my eye as I waited for the starter's gun. Then I was staring at the far end of the pool, every muscle tensed, ready to explode from the blocks.

"Ladies, this is one-hundred-yard freestyle," said the starter. "Take your marks . . ."

My feet were off the blocks as the gun sounded. Fast starts are one of my strong points. The water felt cold as I slapped against it. I am not at my best in cold pools, even though cold water is supposed to be better for records. Being so skinny I feel the cold a lot, and it slows me down. My arms didn't feel any better than they had during warm-up. I was working very hard and going nowhere. As I turned to breathe, I saw the orange cap right beside me.

After the first flip I couldn't see her anymore because I was breathing on the other side, but when we turned again, she was still right there. Had she beaten me in the hundred free in Junior Nationals? I didn't think so, but I couldn't be sure. All my concentration had gone into winning my two fly events. The other events were hazy in my memory. She was there at the last turn. I couldn't let Mark see me beaten in my first race. Immediately my brain switched my body into a higher gear, and with a few yards to go I drove myself into the wall to out-touch her.

"Good race," I said to her as I dragged myself out of the pool. I noticed she looked a lot less tired than I did.

The hundred fly wasn't much of a problem. After all, there are probably only a couple of girls in the country who can beat me at my best. Today, even though I was nowhere near my best, I won easily.

Then came the I.M.—the individual medley. Again Caroline Yee was in the next lane. I have never liked I.M. races, probably because I am forced to swim two lengths of breaststroke in the middle, and that is by far my weakest stroke. As we got to the blocks, I remembered something. I remembered that Caroline Yee had made finals in breaststroke at Junior Nationals.

"Good luck," she said cheerfully. She didn't look at all tired, and I felt ready to fall asleep. The gun sounded, and I worked hard at the two lengths of fly. I had to get a good lead in my best stroke so that I was uncatchable. My backstroke is strong, too, but so was hers. When we turned into the breast, she was only a few yards behind me. I pulled as hard as I could in the breaststroke, but it was no use. Air didn't seem to be reaching my lungs. My lungs felt as if they were on fire. I heard her coming up beside me, gaining on me with every stroke. At the turn we were almost even. On the second length she began to pull away. I was aware of wild cheering from the North supporters. Kids from the South team crowded at the end of the pool to cheer me on.

"Go, Jennie, go. Go, Jennie, go." I could see mouths moving, pleading with me. I flung myself into the freestyle. She was a couple of yards ahead. I thought my arms would drop off, but I was definitely gaining. Her feet were even with my face, then her calves, then her thighs. I turned a fraction of a second after she did and saw in horror that she was putting on a spurt. She had some strength saved for the last length. I had to stay with her. We raced together stroke for stroke down that pool. I tried every trick I could think of to make myself move faster, but my body just refused. Her fingers touched the wall two-tenths of a second ahead of mine.

The North Texans were going wild as we climbed out of the water. Nobody said anything to me. I grabbed my towel and went into the locker room. The future Olympic star had just allowed herself to be beaten in a small state meet.

Chapter 11

"Don't worry about it," Mark said on the way home. "You have a cold, and you lost one race. That's nothing. You won three gold medals in one day. That should keep you happy."

My mother said nothing. She stared straight ahead and drove home tight-lipped. That was far more scary than a mother who yelled. I hadn't even dared face Tod. Usually I had to report to him after each race to discuss how I had swum it. Today I slipped straight into my warm-up suit and went home.

My mother spoke only a few words to me all evening. My father, as usual, thought the whole thing was rather funny.

"So the child wonder got beaten, did she?" he asked, ruffling my hair as he used to when I was a little girl. "Don't take it to heart, Poppet. It happens to the best of us."

"How can you say that, Harry?" snapped my mother in horror. "She must take it to heart. She must learn a lesson from it. Now she knows how it feels to be humiliated. She must say, 'I will never allow that to happen to me again,' and work even harder."

"Cool down, Moira," said my father. "You talk like it's the end of the world, not one lousy swim meet. I don't want my daughter to swim if it's going to make her miserable."

"Well, you wouldn't understand," said my mother. "A champion has to make sacrifices. She has to suffer, too."

"I'm going to bed," I said. I had suffered enough for one day. And no one seemed to know or care that I was sick.

I was almost asleep when the phone rang. I heard my father say, "I'll see if she's awake."

I got phone calls so rarely in the evening that I leaped out of bed. It was Mark, of course.

"Sorry, did I wake you up? I didn't think you'd be in bed at nine."

"It was easier than having my parents fight over me."

"Is your mother still mad?"

"I don't think she'll ever forgive me for as long as I live. She feels she's been humiliated because I lost in Texas."

"You know," said Mark slowly, "sometime you've got to put your foot down. It's your life, after all. You can't let your mother and your coach live it for you. I saw how unhappy you were in the car today. You shouldn't be made to feel like that just because you lost one race. You've got to stand up to them—tell them you're not a racehorse they're training, but a person with feelings. OK?"

"OK," I said hesitantly.

"Say it louder—like you mean it, OK?"

"OK," I said, laughing.

"That's my girl. See you tomorrow. Bye."

"Bye."

I put the phone down in a dream—a warm, cozy dream. Mark was on my side. And had he meant it when he said, "That's my girl"?

Next morning, six A.M. the new Jennie Webster marched up to Tod.

"Well," he said, "what have you got to say for yourself, young lady? You don't improve a single time, and you allow yourself to get beaten! I had your mother on my back all last evening. She called and told me I was to make you work harder. Also, she said she feels that this boyfriend, the former football player, is not such a good idea, after all. She feels he's a bad influence on you. He's taking your mind off your swimming and doesn't seem to realize how important it is."

I think I would have kept my cool fairly well about the whole thing if he hadn't brought Mark into it. As it was, I exploded.

"I am sixteen years old now," I shouted. "It's only natural I should want some sort of life apart from swimming, swimming, swimming. If it means I can't have friends and see them sometimes, then I don't want to swim at all."

Tod put an arm around my shoulder. "Calm down, Jennie. I only meant—"

I shook him off. "No, I won't calm down. Not till I've said what I want to. I want you and my mother to understand something. Nobody else can make me into a champion if I don't want to be one. I'm the only one who can make me swim fast. And if you keep bugging me about every little thing and try to stop me from having friends, then I'll quit. Neither you nor my mother can make me swim if I don't want to!"

Tod's face went pale. "Jennie, honey," he said. "It's OK. I understand. Really I do. I was a swimmer myself, remember? You've had a hard time moving and getting used to a new sort of life here. So have I. But the worst is over, I promise. You've trained for all these years, and now the end is actually in sight. You have a good chance of winning Nationals this spring and making the Olympic team in the summer. You're tired, I know, but don't talk about quitting now—it's all about to happen for you." He looked really scared, as if he knew he was about to lose his one Olympic prospect. I couldn't help feeling sorry for him. But I also felt good—it was the first time I felt I had power over him.

"Don't worry, Tod," I said quietly. "I don't really want to quit. I just want you to understand that I'm a big girl now. I want to run my own life. You know I'm sensible—I'm not about to go to any all-night parties or start smoking pot. Just let me do what I think is best."

Tod obviously got my message and equally obviously had a little talk with my mother during the day, because when I got home from school that afternoon she was also extra-understanding. She even said she realized how tired I was and what a strain the move had been on all of us.

Thank you, Mark, I thought as I fell asleep. *If it hadn't been for you, I would never have dared to say those things.*

The world sure feels different when you have someone standing beside you.

Chapter 12

All the same, I couldn't help feeling down in the dumps about my swimming. If I couldn't win in Texas, what was going to happen in the Nationals? I knew that some girls peaked at fourteen or even younger. Could it be that I was already past my best and wasn't ever going to get any better? Did I have a long downhill slide to look forward to? It was not a comforting thought to wonder if you were a has-been at sixteen.

It was a gray time of year. It rained a lot—cold downpours that soaked you in seconds and turned the ground into a lake so that your shoes were permanently squishy. There were often great flashes of lightning and loud claps of thunder that rattled whole buildings and scared me half to death. When Texans kept asking me if I hadn't been afraid of earthquakes all the time in California, I told them that I had never been afraid of them like I was of their thunderstorms. They thought this was very funny, but then I thought their earthquake fear was just as funny, too!

Another thing that was bugging me was how Mark always managed to sidestep my suggestion that he start swimming.

"I'll think about it" and "Don't rush me" were his favorite expressions. I didn't want to be too pushy—so it looked as though he would never be ready to give up those crutches.

And worst of all, the holiday season was coming up. Lights appeared on buildings and lampposts. Store windows bulged with Christmas merchandise. Every time I watched TV there was some commercial about coming home for the holidays and being with your family. These would be the first holidays I had ever spent away from my relatives in California.

On Thanksgiving we always went to Grandma Webster's house. She had a small, white frame house in the middle of Santa Barbara, and when my family and Uncle Danny's family and Aunt Sue's family all tried to fit in at once, it was a tight squeeze. But we managed somehow. The weather was usually good, so Grandma put a picnic table up on the patio for the kids, and we had lots of fun being rude to one another out of earshot of the adults.

I thought of Thanksgiving with just the three of us in the huge, elegant house. Mother said it was hardly worth buying a turkey just for three and steaks would make a nice change.

We called Grandma Webster on Thanksgiving morning.

"Is that my little Jennie?" she asked as usual, although I have been taller than she since I was ten. Then she chatted on about the number of jars of fruit she had put up, the things she was making for the Christmas bazaar at church, and the pies she had baked for today. "And you should see the turkey. Uncle Danny won it in a raffle, and it is bigger than your cousin Kimberly. It just fits in the oven, and I spent all yesterday making stuffing to go in it. We're sure going to miss you and your appetite. Now who will finish it up for me? Your cousin Angela's no use. She told me she's on a diet, and she won't eat anything except salad. A diet! I ask you—did you ever hear about a fourteen-year-old girl on a diet?"

I could see my mother making signs to me to hurry up. Grandma always managed to forget that long-distance calls cost more money than calls across Santa Barbara. She asked me about swimming and told me to call her when I was in California for Nationals. She was just about to tell me about the new roof she had had put on her house when I interrupted.

"Grandma, I'm sorry but I have to go. Mother's saying the call will cost more than flying out to see you."

"Oh, I wish you could all do that." She sighed.

"I wish it, too, Grandma," I said.

After I had put the phone down, I felt sadder than ever. Suddenly it seemed that nothing nice would ever happen again.

A few days later, something nice did happen. At Oak Creek High they announced things over the PA system during homeroom every morning: scholarships students had won, sports or games they had done well in, things like that. I never really listened too closely. I was always tired after swimming, and I hardly ever knew the kids. So I was working on my chemistry homework, due sixth period but somehow not finished, when I heard: "Mark Waverly—winner of the Texas High School Art Award. A great accomplishment for Mark and a great honor for Oak Creek High!"

I had always believed he could win, but I had never dreamed it would be shouted out in public like that. Had Mark known beforehand, or was it news to him over the loudspeaker, too? I hardly dared to face him at lunchtime. I saw him come into the cafeteria, and I couldn't tell if he looked mad or not. After all, he had every right to be mad. He'd probably never speak to me again. Or he'd yell at me in front of the whole cafeteria.

I was holding my breath as he sat down beside me.

"I guess you heard," he said.

I nodded. "Congratulations."

He looked at me very strangely. "Very funny thing that I find that I win a contest I didn't even enter. I guess someone must have entered for me—and it wouldn't take too many brains to figure out who. There's only one person who has seen all my drawings."

"Mark, are you mad at me? I knew you'd never enter the contest, and I knew that your work was good enough to win—"

"Whether I won or not is beside the point.

The fact is that you're trying to run my life for me."

"Mark, I'm not. Honestly, I'm not. I only wanted to help—I just felt that you needed a little ego boost."

"Well, thanks. I've now been announced to the whole school as a weirdo who wins art contests. Do you think anyone else will think that is anything worth shouting about?"

Mark's voice was pretty loud. I saw people turning around to look at us, and I felt myself blushing again. A group of kids walked past us. I hunched down in my misery. They stopped at our table.

"Hey, Mark," one of them said. "That was great news. I'd no idea you were an artist."

"Congratulations, Mark."

"Hey, Mark, you're a sly one, keeping talent like that to yourself."

"Mark, how about designing the cover for the yearbook this year?"

Mark shrugged them off, but I could see he was pleased.

After they had gone, I couldn't resist asking, "By the way, what were you saying before we were interrupted?" And Mark couldn't help grinning a little.

By the end of the day it was clear that Mark had gotten things all wrong. The kids did think that he had done something pretty important. They didn't think it was weird or odd. Even people he didn't know came up to him and said nice things. At the end of school he was called into the principal's office.

He call me as soon as he got home. "I bet you want to know what Mr. Griffith said this afternoon. He wants me to design a mural for the entrance hall."

"Wow, Mark. That's fantastic. Did you say you would?"

"Well, I could hardly say no to the principal, could I?"

"Mark?" I asked. "Are you still mad at me?"

"How could I be? Just do me a favor, OK? If you're going to run my life, just keep me informed. I'll see you tomorrow. And, Jennie, thanks. For everything."

Chapter 13

Mark got busy on the mural design right away. He had decided on a picture of a Texas ranch with longhorn cattle and a windmill. He had also planned lots of details of Texas wildlife. After he had done the sketch, the art teacher helped him project it onto the wall. Then a group of kids from art class did most of the actual painting. Mark was there all his spare time. He supervised the bits he couldn't reach and did the details, such as bluebonnet flowers and armadillos, himself.

I began to see less of him. He hardly ever came into the cafeteria for lunch. Instead, he grabbed a sandwich while he was working on the mural. And when I did see him, he was usually surrounded by the group of kids who were helping with the painting. There were a lot of cute girls in the group, and I felt a stupid pang of jealousy as I watched them joking with Mark.

One day I was passing the mural, and there was Mark, dressed in paint-spattered overalls, joking with a cute little blond who looked even cuter because she was wearing a huge man's shirt covered with paint splotches. Her hair was kept out of the way in two little blond braids, making her look like a ten-year-old. As I came toward them, Mark's back was to me, and I saw him put a dab of blue paint on the tip of her nose. She squealed in mock anger and said, "I'll get you for that, Mark Waverly," in a voice that carried a thousand hints.

I hurried to the cafeteria without even stopping to say hi. I chewed furiously while the thoughts raced around my head just as furiously.

"Now you've done it," I said to myself. "You wanted to help Mark get back into the swing of things. You wanted him to get back his self-confidence and find a new interest. Well, you've done all that and look what's happened. Now he doesn't need you. Let's face it—he never did think of you as a girl at all. You were just someone who happened to be there. You're not pretty and sexy, and you don't know how to flirt like those girls do—"

I really hadn't realized how much he had meant to me until now. The thought of sharing him with the other kids, of watching him with a new girlfriend, perhaps, was too painful to bear. If I couldn't have Mark, then I didn't want to swim or stay in Texas one minute longer. The trouble was that if I had lost him, I didn't know how to go about getting him back.

He probably still hasn't forgiven me for entering him in the competition, *I thought miserably.* Even though the competition was good for him, he's probably still mad at me, even if he says he's not.

The mural was finished before Christmas. Reporters came from several papers and took pictures of Mark beside the mural. Then stories appeared saying, "Former football star discovers new talent. . . ." I don't know what Mark thought of them. I was never alone with him enough to find out.

When I did see him, he was nice and even said, "I never get to see you these days." But he didn't suggest when he could get to see me, and when he had gone, I felt more down than ever.

The day after the grand unveiling of the mural with all the school board present, Mark still didn't come to the cafeteria for lunch. I heard from a girl in math that he had changed his schedule and his lunch period was not the same as mine. "Now I know that he wants to stay clear of me," I mumbled to myself and walked alone through the halls in black depression.

As I passed the famous mural, I stopped to look at it.

"It's all your fault," I told it, but I couldn't help admiring its beauty. Mark's drawings had all been in black and white. This painting in full color was spectacular as well as beautiful.

"Admiring your boyfriend's work?" drawled a voice behind me. Luanne was standing there with some of her crowd. They looked amused. I didn't know what to say. So I said nothing.

"So Mark's made a great comeback into the

headlines," said Luanne sweetly. "And all thanks to you, I hear. Pretty soon he'll be quite recovered, and you'll be able to live happily ever after." The friends giggled, but Luanne didn't.

"Of course, he's becoming very popular again," Luanne went on. "You'll have to watch that—little Sue Oppenheim from art class thinks he's real cute, and he always hurries off somewhere after school every day. I wonder where he goes. You wouldn't happen to know, would you?"

"It's none of my business where Mark goes after school and none of yours, either," I said and tried to walk past her.

"Oh, come on now," Luanne said, barring my way. "Everyone knows about you and Mark. Don't pretend you don't care if he's meeting Sue Oppenheim after school."

I was angry now and confused, too. Of course I cared, but I wasn't going to let Luanne know that.

"Look, Luanne," I said. "Get one thing straight, will you? Mark is not my boyfriend."

"Oh, I see," she said, sneering. "And all that time you spent with him—even going to his house, I hear—was only because you felt sorry for him, because you wanted to help a poor cripple. No personal feelings involved, right?"

I decided to get her off my back once and for all. "That's right," I said. "I helped him because I felt sorry for him. I have no personal feelings for Mark Waverly whatsoever."

I turned toward the main entrance and saw Mark standing there. The look on his face told me right away that he had heard. He stared at me for a moment with a look of unbelieving hurt. Then he turned and went out through the main door.

I pushed Luanne out of the way and ran after him.

"Mark, wait!" I called.

Outside, the good old Texas rain was coming down. Mark seemed not to notice it as he hurried down the front path. Thunder was grumbling somewhere beyond the trees.

"Mark, please wait," I called above the drumming of the rain and the growl of thunder. But he didn't even turn around. I rushed out into the rain after him. It was coming down so fiercely that it took my breath away. I caught up with him at the end of the path and grabbed his arm.

"Mark, please listen to me—"

"I listened to you already," he said bitterly. "Back there in the hall. Well, you can go and take your good deeds somewhere else, Miss Do-Gooder—because I don't need you or your pity."

"Mark, I didn't mean those things." I started to cry, but you couldn't see the tears because of the rain streaming down my face.

"Like hell you didn't. You must feel very proud of yourself—rehabilitating the handicapped, getting poor old Mark interested in occupational therapy. I suppose you've been boasting all over school how you sent my picture in to the contest for me—to get me on my feet again!"

"Mark, that's not true. You must know that I wouldn't be like that. I only said those things to get Luanne to leave me alone. She was saying lots of mean, spiteful things about how you were interested in Sue Oppenheim. I didn't want her to see how much I cared."

"Sue Oppenheim?" Mark said suddenly. "That little squirt? What did she say about Sue Oppenheim?"

"That you and she—you know—" I broke off with a sob.

Mark's lips twitched in a smile. "Sue Oppenheim and me? You were worried about Sue Oppenheim and me?" The smile turned into a grin.

"Mark—I never get to see you anymore. I thought you didn't need me, that I wouldn't get to see you again. And I couldn't bear to think of it."

"Do you really care about me like that?" he asked. Before I could answer, there was a great flash of lightning close by, followed almost immediately by a giant crash of thunder. I think I let out a little scream of terror. Almost before I knew it, I was in his arms. He had dropped his crutches, and his strong arms were holding me tight.

"It's OK," he whispered into my hair. "We didn't get hit."

"Oh, Mark," I said, nestling my head against his shoulder, "I love you so much. . . ."

He held me away from him so that he could look into my face. "What did you say?" he asked.

"I think I said that I love you," I said shakily.

"Oh, Jennie," he said. Then he kissed me, and in spite of the rain, his lips were warm against mine.

When the lightning and thunder came again, we hardly noticed it.

"I think," Mark said after a while, "that we ought to move away from these trees. Now that we've found each other I, for one, don't want to get barbecued by lightning." Then he kissed me again lightly, on my forehead.

"Here, hand me those things," he said, looking with distaste at the crutches. As I picked them up, he went on, "I sure hope I'll be able to do without them soon. They're a damn nuisance. For instance, if I only had my car at school, we could both slip away together now and forget about this afternoon's classes."

The rosy glow was beginning to wear off, and I realized that I was soaked to the skin. My clothes were clinging to me like sodden rags, and my hair was plastered to my cheeks.

"Mark," I said in horror, "we can't go back to school like this. I couldn't possibly go into chemistry class like a drowned rat. What are we going to do?"

"I guess I could call home," he said. "Someone's usually there."

"Well, my mother's in Houston for the day," I said, sighing in relief. I wouldn't have enjoyed explaining what I was doing out in a thunderstorm.

"Come on," he said. "Let's go phone from

the gym. There's a pay phone in the hall. That way we don't have to go back into school at all."

We waded side by side toward the gym. Every now and then we would turn and look at each other with happy grins, as if we shared a private joke the rest of the world didn't know.

Mark made his phone call and luckily his father was home. We huddled together at the entrance of the gym, waiting for the car to come.

"I hope they hurry up," I said, shivering.

"I don't," Mark said, drawing me toward him. "I can think of a really good way to pass the time."

Then he kissed me again. It was much better with no rain pounding on my face. *My first real kiss*, I thought. Yet it didn't feel strange. Isn't it funny that you know how without being taught!

"Mark," I said, a little breathlessly. My legs were feeling like jelly, and it wasn't from the cold and rain. "I want to ask you something. When did you first . . . start feeling like this about me?"

He smiled. "Oh, I can tell you when I first fell in love with you. It was when you jumped up and down like a crazy thing at the football game and almost fell off the bleachers."

"Then why didn't you tell me before?"

"I've been through a rough time, Jennie. After the accident, I got suspicious of everybody. I thought they all felt sorry for me—and I was frightened of being hurt some more. When I was with you, I made myself play it cool because I wasn't sure of you—I wasn't sure right up till now. There were several times when I nearly told you how I felt—but I kept remembering the way you swim. You are the kind of athlete I used to be, and I couldn't see how you'd want to be stuck with someone who would never be an athlete again."

"Oh, Mark—you are an idiot. It doesn't matter in the least to me if someone's a football player or a stamp collector. Suppose you were terrified of water—would you still love me even though I'm a swimmer?"

"Now y'all just confusin' a poor Texas farm boy," he said in a mock drawl. "But you know what—I wish my folks would hurry up now. Jeans feel terrible when they are cold and wet."

As if on cue, Mark's father arrived. He was an enormous man, who looked like an artist's cartoon of a Texas farmer—complete with hat, belt, and boots. He eyed us up and down as if he were looking at two creatures newly arrived from Mars.

"Well," he said, "what do we have here?"

Chapter 14

Did I say that I was dreading the most depressing Christmas ever? Let me take that back right now. It turned out to be the most wonderful, fantastic, unbelievable Christmas ever experienced by a human being since the year one.

How different the shopping centers looked, as if someone had redecorated them when I wasn't looking. Only a week before, my mother had dragged me around the big, new mall near us to buy presents to send back to California. I hated everything about it. The windows were full of shiny electronic toys that were going to need new batteries after two days. There were hideous Christmas hostess outfits with gold lamé tops and gross little aprons to pin on when you served appetizers. Worst of all were the fake Christmas trees made of aluminum and vinyl. At home we always had a real tree brought down from the forests only a week or so before and smelling green and Christmasy. My mother paused by the artificial trees until I told her that over my dead body would we have an artificial tree in the house.

"Then I guess it will have to be no tree at all," she said stiffly. "Have you seen how much they want for fresh trees down here? It would be cheaper to fly to the Rockies and cut down our own."

"Let's do that!" I said excitedly.

"Jennie, sometimes I wonder if you are ever going to grow up." She sighed. My mother had obviously never been born a little girl. She had been born practical and sensible and grown up.

She launched into one of her favorite topics: "Do you realize how much it is costing to train you as a swimmer? Do you know how many suits and caps you go through in a year? Then there is the air fare and hotel bills for the Nationals coming up. That won't be cheap, either. And you have the nerve to talk about flying to cut down a Christmas tree."

"Forget it," I had said, and stumbled ahead so blindly that I was trampled down by a fat family—father all hat, boots, and stomach hanging over his belt; mother all teased, bleached hair in a beehive and having an equally fat stomach; and kids, runny-nosed and also fat.

"I hate Texas!" I had repeated to myself three hundred times.

Now, a week later, I went back to that same mall with Mark. Had someone really sneaked in without telling me and rearranged it into a wonderland? How come I had managed to miss the snowflakes sparkling from the ceiling or the window full of darling puppies or the little china frogs or the beautiful seashells?

And where were all the horrible fat people? The only families I saw today were nice-looking, laughing, well-dressed parents with cute, chubby kids, who were as wide-eyed with the wonder of the season as I felt.

It seemed that being in love with Mark had opened the doorway to miracles. When I complained that we didn't even have a Christmas tree and my folks were threatening to buy a plastic one, he just laughed.

"Is that all you need to make you happy—a Christmas tree? That's easily taken care of," he said, looking smug. "We have lots of cedars in the forest at the back of our property. They make great Christmas trees. We'll get one of the ranch hands to drive us out there in the Jeep and cut one down for you."

And so we did, a week before Christmas. It was early in the morning. The air was crisp and smelled of wood smoke, and the sky was as blue as in California. The horrible, swampy Texas forest full of snakes and spiders and skinny trees had vanished, thanks to Mark the magician, and in its place had grown a world of Spanish moss and squirrels and bright-red cardinals. I spent an excited half hour running from one cedar to the next, thinking I had chosen the perfect one, then seeing another more perfect one through the trees. Mark beamed to see me so happy, as if he had grown the trees personally for my delight.

Mark was coming over for lunch on Christmas Day. Surprisingly, my family had not made a fuss about him. Perhaps they had seen me walking three feet above the ground and realized there was no way that they could pull me down again. It was even my mother who suggested that he come to Christmas lunch—which goes to show that either miracles can happen or my mother is a bigger softie than I had ever imagined.

I had agonized over what to give Mark for Christmas. Part of me wanted to play it safe and give him art supplies or clothes, and part of me wanted to go the whole hog and get him some jewelry that said "Jennie and Mark." I think the cautious side of me would have won, except I saw the most perfect plain bracelet in silver at our local jewelry store. Before I could stop myself, I was telling the clerk, "I want it engraved Jennie and Mark." Once the engraving machine started, there was no going back.

I had a few nervous moments thinking about giving it to him, but I kept telling myself, "After all, he doesn't have to wear it."

I showed it to my parents on Christmas Eve. I wished I hadn't.

"A bracelet for a boy?" asked my father in horror.

"Boys wear that sort of thing these days," my mother said. But I still felt a nagging doubt that I was doing the right thing.

Christmas morning was another beautiful, clear day. Was I imagining things, or had it not rained since Mark had taken over the world? We all opened our presents—none too imaginative. Mine were clothes and two records and a stuffed alligator to add to the stuffed-animal collection at the end of my bed. Most of the California relatives had sent money instead of presents. Although money is nice, it is not as much fun as ripping off wrapping paper on Christmas morning.

About ten-thirty Mark arrived. I met him at the front door.

"Where's the mistletoe?" he asked.

"We don't have any."

"Oh, well, I guess we'll just have to manage without," he said, kissing me right there in the doorway.

"You want to come and get your present?" he asked, looking mysterious and pleased with himself. "It's out in the car."

"OK," I said, and we walked back to the car together.

"It's in the back seat," said Mark, looking as excited as I felt.

I put my hand on the car door—and finally the gears started to move in my brain. "This is your car!"

He nodded.

"You drove yourself over here!"

"Right."

I opened the back door. On the seat, tied up with red and green ribbons, were the crutches. I hadn't even noticed that he was walking without them.

"Actually I could walk pretty well without them a couple of weeks ago, but I wanted to surprise you for Christmas!" he said.

I couldn't find anything to say. I just gaped.

He laughed. "Well, I guess I surprised you.

You were right about the swimming. It worked very well, as you can see."

"But you never came," I stammered. "You kept putting it off."

"That's what I told you! I didn't want to swim at your center and have your coach and all the team staring at me making a fool of myself. So I got the high-school coach to let me work out after school in the school pool." He put an arm around me. "And you know what? I'm getting pretty good. I think I'll be able to beat you soon!"

We laughed together as we walked back from the car. Inside the house I handed him his present.

"Oh, here," he said. "This is the rest of yours." And he gave me a small, slim box. We opened them at the same time, and both burst out laughing. Mark's gift to me was a silver bracelet engraved Jennie and Mark.

Chapter 15

Every other year I remember waking up the day after Christmas and thinking nothing nice would ever happen to me again. This year it was very hard to believe that, with Mark's red TransAm pulling up for me outside the house and my new bracelet feeling heavy and comforting on my wrist.

I was even allowed to take a couple of days off from swimming. I had the sheer joy of sleeping until it was light. Actually my body and mind were so used to waking early that I woke with a start at five-fifteen and had a moment's panic that my alarm had not gone off. Then I remembered, heaved a huge, contented sigh, and fell back to sleep again.

Then it was back to swimming, and I came down to reality with a bump. On the first morning back, December 28, Tod called me into his office, a thing he never did. The coach's office was a tiny glass cubicle at one end of the indoor pool. It was so cluttered with kickboards, meet entry cards, whistles, sweatshirts, pull buoys, paddles, old coffee cups, umbrellas, and all the other items a coach needs to survive that there was hardly room for me to squeeze in.

"Sit down, Jennie," Tod said, pushing some papers off the spare chair.

This sounded serious. Adults usually asked you to sit down only when they had some bad news for you.

"Jennie, you and I have got to talk about Nationals."

I nodded, my heart thumping and wondering what was coming next.

"Do you realize that Nationals are only just over two months away?"

Of course I realized it. I'd even been crossing off days on my calendar.

"And do you realize that since coming to Texas, you haven't improved a single time?"

I nodded. "But I've hardly been to any meets."

"It's not just meets," Tod said. "You aren't looking as good in practice as you were in Santa Barbara."

"You don't realize how hard it is for me here," I blurted out. "I have no one to pace me, no one to compete with, and I have to wait while little kids finish sets of hundreds on the two minutes. How am I supposed to improve when I'm swimming all on my own like that?"

Tod nodded as he played with a dish of paper clips on his desk. "I know it hasn't been easy for you. In fact, I've been feeling very bad about bringing you here. I thought—well, I thought things would be a little different. I thought there would be some more talent on the team. I thought I'd have the assistant coach they promised me—but they won't give me one until we have over fifty swimmers on the team—and we'll never have more than fifty swimmers until we can teach these Texans that there are other sports besides football!

"Anyway, those are all my problems—they shouldn't have to be your problems, too. But I have to say this—Texas was a wrong move for you. You have a great future in swimming, and I can't see you making it if you stay with me."

He paused and looked up at me. "What I'm trying to say, Jennie, is that I think you should go back to California right away. I've talked to Snyder at Mission Viejo, and he says he'll take you. He'll even find a family for you to board with if your parents can't move back right away."

I stared at him like a zombie. "You want me to go back to California? Now?"

"If you want to win Nationals."

"But my parents have just gone through all this trouble to move here. I've had to adjust to a new high school—and you want us to go through all that again?" I was squeaking now like a frustrated mouse.

"Jennie—I don't know what to say. Everything you've said about there being no challenge for you on this team is true. It's very hard for you to improve in a vacuum like this. Please, go home, tell your parents what I've said, and think about it carefully."

I went home in a daze. How strange the world was. Only a few weeks ago I would have done anything to get back to California. Now I was being offered a chance to train with the best team in the nation, in a place where I longed to be—and I didn't want to go. It didn't need any thinking over. I had made up my mind long before I reached the front door: if I had to give up swimming or Mark, I'd give up swimming any day.

So I didn't even mention it to my parents. After all, they had given up a lot to come to Texas. They were both native Californians with all their roots in Santa Barbara. My father had had to do a lot of fighting to get accepted in his new job, and things seemed to be going better for him now. At least he was not biting our heads off as much at home, which was a good sign.

But I did tell Mark. When you love somebody, it is very hard to keep secrets from them. He looked very worried.

"I think you should go," he said at last.

"You want me to go?" I asked, feeling confused and hurt.

"Of course I don't want you to. It's the last thing in the whole world I want. But I don't want to stand in your way, either. If winning Nationals means a lot to you and you're really not improving here, then you should go where you can improve. I'm just trying to look at it calmly and logically."

"But, Mark, I want to be where you are. If I was far away from you, you don't think I could swim well, do you?"

Mark smiled. "Typical woman," he said. "Much too emotional."

Then I hit him, and he grabbed my wrists, and for a time we forgot about any bigger problems.

But the problem did not go away. I lay awake at nights wrestling with it. Of course I wanted to win Nationals. Of course I wanted to train at Mission Viejo. Of course I wanted to be with Mark. There didn't seem to be any solution, apart from taking Mark with me or bringing Mission Viejo here.

In the meantime I told Tod I was still thinking about it and vowed to work so hard that he would decide it was all right for me to stay after all. The only really good thing that had happened was that there were no more car pools. Mark offered to drive me down every day and did his homework in the snack bar while I swam.

"Why don't you bring a suit and work out too tomorrow?" I suggested. "I've never seen you swim yet."

"OK, maybe I will," he said. "But I'm going to swim indoors where you can't see how badly I do it."

That's what he did, too. He joined me for the weightlifting (and was very good at it) and then disappeared to the indoor pool.

At the end of workout he came out wrapped in his towel to see if I was finished. I almost was finished, too—it had been a hard workout that day, and I had worked extra-hard. I was lying against the side of the pool when Mark saw me.

"Right," he said, a gleam in his eyes, peeling off his towel. "You look good and tired. I'll race you down the pool."

"That's not fair. I can hardly move."

"That makes things more even."

"Mark, I couldn't race now. I'm beat."

"Afraid I might win?" he teased.

"OK. I guess I can swim one more length," I said wearily.

"Take your marks, go," he shouted as he dived in over my head. He was swimming ahead of me, thrashing up the water like a drowning man, but I had to admit he was pretty fast. His powerful shoulders and arms had been made more powerful by those months on crutches, and I had to swim hard to catch him. It was not easy to swim with the faceful of water that his splashing produced. I think I could have out-touched him if I had really tried, but as it was we came in side by side, storming into the end of the pool. Right at Tod's feet.

"Hey," he said, grinning. "Met your match at last, eh?"

Tod squatted down to Mark. "Did you ever think of joining the team?" he said, a glint in his eye. "Your style is terrible, but you certainly have the power. I could make you into a good swimmer, and if Jennie had you here," he added, "maybe you'd help her to work out harder."

Chapter 16

So Mark joined the team, and right away I could feel the difference in my swimming. Of course he wasn't good enough to give me any competition, but while he was building up his own stamina, Tod used him to help coach me.

"Your breaststroke leg in the I.M. was too weak again," he would say, checking the watch. "You've got to take two seconds off that." He would take my pulse during sprints to see if I was swimming too tired. Best of all was just the knowledge that he was there to share in my training. It made a world of difference, and I started to enjoy my swimming again. Tod stopped bugging me about Mission Viejo.

I'd forgotten what fun it was to have someone to share things with, to climb into the car and say, "Wasn't Tod in a foul mood tonight?" and "What intervals did you do your sprints on?" and "Wasn't the water freezing tonight?"

Mark also worked hard at his own swimming and quickly improved. Tod started him off in one of the humble lanes to the left of me with the little kids, and every few days he would be moved up one lane closer to me.

"Wait till you have me in your lane, I'll make you work, all right," he threatened me. It turned out that with his height, he was a natural backstroker and could soon give me a run for my money in that stroke as well as in freestyle. But he remained frustrated about butterfly. Fly is a really hard stroke to learn if you are not a child, and Mark was no exception.

"How on earth do you manage to fit the kicks with your arms?" he asked, annoyed when he saw me laughing at his fly stroke. "I have to keep struggling to keep from sinking."

"Yes, I noticed," I said, trying to stifle my giggles. "You see, you're trying to kick at the same time as you pull. You need one kick when your arms are by your hips and one when they are straight in front of you."

But he still couldn't get it.

"You'll never be able to swim an I.M. if you don't learn fly," I challenged.

"Then I'll go through life never swimming an I.M.," he retorted. "There are worse things that could happen to me than never swimming an I.M."

But I noticed that he practiced fly when he thought I wasn't looking.

At the end of January I entered a senior meet in Louisiana and was first in everything I swam. I took two seconds off my I.M., which Mark looked upon as a personal victory for him, and everyone was pleased afterward.

Also at the end of January, something almost unheard of happened. The weather had been bleak and cold, with bitter winds that froze your body numb as soon as you climbed out of the water. Then one morning I woke up to a strange glow in my room. I lay there staring at the ceiling and the window, trying to figure out what could be lighting my room two hours before dawn. But I was too warm and comfortable to get out of bed and look. When finally curiosity got the better of me and I went over to the window, I got a tremendous shock. It had snowed! Snow in South Texas is something that never happens. We're on the same latitude as Egypt, and the climate is meant to be subtropical.

I went downstairs to find my mother already dressed but walking around like a zombie, putting out coffee mugs. The radio was blaring out cheerful good-morning music.

"No school," my mother muttered in her zombie voice.

"What?" I thought I hadn't heard right.

"That's what they just said on the radio. All schools in North Houston closed due to snow."

"But it only looks like a sprinkling. Are the roads closed?"

"Don't ask me—it appears that school buses are unable to drive through the least hint of snow. I am not such a nervous Nellie. I shall drive to swimming this morning, snow or no snow."

"I thought you would. I bet you would dig

us out of a blizzard so that I didn't miss my swimming."

"Well, you know what the mailmen say about neither snow nor sleet nor hail. . . . The same goes for me. Have some coffee."

My mother poured me a big mug, and I sloshed a whole lot of cream and sugar into it, which made her shudder as usual.

The roads weren't all that bad, and the snow wasn't thick, so swimming was fun. There were shapeless white mounds all around us, melting at the edges as they met the steam from the pool.

When I got home, I saw my father's car still there.

"I see you didn't dare brave the blizzard," I teased him, and gave him a kiss.

"I have a good excuse to stay home," he said. "I am waiting for an important call from California."

The snow made me extra hungry, and I tackled a second breakfast of pancakes and bacon. I had almost finished when Mark called.

"Of course I know it snowed," I said in a very superior voice. "Have you just woken up? I've already been to morning workout!"

"I'll see you in a few minutes," he said. "Go get your warm clothes on. We're going skiing."

"We're what?"

"Going skiing."

"You've got to be crazy. I know there's snow out there, but I have to break the bad news to you—there are no hills in South Texas."

"Trust me," he said. "Now don't stand around arguing, woman. Go get your skis ready, and I'll see you in a few minutes."

"What are you looking for, dear?" my mother called as she heard me clomping around in the attic.

"My ski boots. Mark's taking me skiing," I called back.

"In South Texas?" said my mother. "He's got to be out of his mind, that boy. The boots are in the green suitcase."

Mark arrived as I was buckling them in the front hall. He looked like a ski pro in a blue and white hat with a white pom-pom on it, a big blue parka, and red ski boots.

"Ready for the downhill run?" he asked.

I laughed. "You're crazy. I'm ready, but I don't think Texas is."

"You wait," he said. "Get in the car and you'll see."

He put my skis up on the roof rack beside his, then we drove off through the white, silent world. We drove through the forest, which had been turned into a Christmas card landscape. Then Mark drove through the main entrance of the big country club near us. We drove right past the clubhouse, along the golf course, and finally Mark parked under some trees.

"OK, where's the hill?" I asked.

"Did it never occur to you that golf courses are not flat?" he said smugly. "This particular green has a good slope on the other side. By Texas standards, this is a long downhill run."

The ski slope proved to be about thirty feet of golf course going away from the green.

As Mark put on his skis, I got a guilty conscience.

"We can't ski on someone's golf course," I said, looking around nervously.

"Well, they can't play golf on it today," Mark said, fastening his ski bindings. "And anyway, my family belongs to this club so I have every right to be here. Come on, scaredy cat!"

And he stomped off to the crest of our giant hill.

"I hope I still remember how to ski," he said, gliding effortlessly to the bottom. The run took all of twenty seconds. Then, giggling like idiots, we marched all the way up to the top again. After a few runs, the novelty wore off, and we started doing crazy things like skiing down backward or holding hands. "Let's go down on one leg only this time," Mark suggested. "When I say go, we'll lift the other ski."

We stood at the top of the hill. "Ready, steady, go—" he yelled. We both lifted one ski, traveled a few yards, swung together out of control, and landed in a heap on the cold, hard turf.

"Mark," I cried as soon as I could breathe properly. "How's your leg? You haven't hurt it, have you?"

"Well, now," he said, moving so that he pinned me down in the snow. "I think I'm just fine all over, thank you, ma'am." Then he kissed me.

"I think you tripped me up on purpose," I said a while later.

"Well, the skiing was getting kinda boring," he admitted.

Then I stuffed some snow in his face, and there was more snowball fighting and more kissing.

At last we drove home, soaking wet, freezing cold, and giggling like first-graders.

"I won't come in," Mark said. "I better get on home and put on some dry clothes before this turns to double pneumonia." He thought for a moment, then said, "Have you realized that the highlights of our relationship have taken place in wet clothes?"

"What can you expect if you date a swimmer?" I laughed, gave him a goodbye kiss, and ran into the house.

I opened the front door, then remembered my snowy boots and sat down on the doormat to take them off. I heard my father's voice coming from the open living-room door. I didn't pay much attention to what he was saying until I heard my mother interrupt. "For heaven's sake don't say anything about it to her until after Nationals."

I pricked up my ears immediately.

"But I always thought she wanted it as much as any of us," said my father.

"That was before she met Mark," said my mother.

"But surely these boy-girl relationships don't last long at her age," said my father. "She'll have forgotten all about him in a couple of months."

"I wouldn't be so sure of that," said my mother. "This is the first real boyfriend she has had, and I think they're pretty serious about each other."

I was now dying of curiosity. I couldn't figure out what in the world they were talking about. What could they not want me to know until after Nationals? Why would they want me to get over Mark? All I could think of was that they had found a boy they thought was more suitable, but that didn't really sound like my parents. I just had to go in and find out. They both looked guilty when they saw me.

"Oh, hello, dear. I didn't hear you come in," said my mother.

"Have a good time?" asked my father. "You look as if you bathed in the snow." He tried to sound cheerful, but he didn't fool me for a minute. He looked worried.

"OK, out with it," I said, facing them both. "I was taking off my boots in the front hall, and I couldn't help overhearing. What couldn't you tell me until after Nationals?"

"Oh, dear," said my mother. "What bad timing. I really didn't want you to know. It's only going to upset you, I know it is."

"What's going to upset me, for pete's sake?" I begged.

"Jennie, honey," said my father, putting an arm around my shoulder. "My old company was on the phone from California this morning.

They haven't managed to find anybody who can replace me, and they have begged me to come back."

"They want you to go back to California?" I said. I felt as if I had just stepped into an elevator that was crashing down from the top floor.

"You're a young woman now," said my father. "I think you must have noticed that I haven't been happy with this new company. I don't enjoy working under so much pressure. Your mother is still a bit lonely in Texas, and up to a few weeks ago, we thought that you weren't happy here, either."

"So we're going to go back?" My voice cracked as I said it.

"They've made a very generous offer. I think I'd be a fool to refuse it. They have even said I could work out of L.A. so you could go to Mission Viejo. You've always wanted to do that, haven't you? They are the best team in the country, aren't they?"

I nodded miserably.

My mother patted my hand. "As things are at the moment, training at Mission Viejo would give you your best chance to make the Olympic squad, wouldn't it?"

I nodded again, and before I could stop it, a tear squeezed itself out of my eye and rolled down my cheek.

"Don't cry, honey," my father said. "We know how you feel about Mark. It's hard for you, but it's not as bad as you think. I don't have to let the company know for a while yet. A lot may happen in a few months."

"You think I'll have gotten over Mark by then," I sobbed, the tears all rushing out at once, "but I won't. I won't forget him ever!"

I rushed to my room and flung myself onto the bed, wet, snowy clothes and all.

Chapter 17

Needless to say, I was not feeling too cool, calm, and collected as February turned into March. Nationals were only a couple of weeks away, and then I had to face another move, another swim team, another coach, another car pool, and no Mark. There didn't seem to be any way I could face it. I tossed it around inside my head, wondering if I could arrange to stay with a family here for my final high-school year, wondering if I could persuade my family to put the move off for a year, wondering. . . . Of course, in the end the whole thing came back to Mark. Mark was a senior, after all. He hadn't decided what he wanted to do next year, but it would surely mean going off to college, perhaps somewhere far away. And of course, in the back of my mind was the thought that Mark might find someone else instead of me one day. I didn't like to think about that.

I'm sure Mark found me quick-tempered, but he put it down to pre-National nerves. So did Tod. He even commented on it. "Just relax, will you, Jennie? You're wearing yourself out. Just remember that this is only a test for you, and nobody expects much from you. Everything you do will be a surprise, so there's no pressure for you to win. Even if you don't come in in the top three, there's always summer Nationals coming up before Olympic selection."

"A couple of months ago you made these Nationals sound like the end of the world."

"That's because you weren't in this jumpy state two months ago. Then you got my get-up-and-get-going speech. Today I'm giving you my calming-down-hyper-swimmer speech."

I grinned—something I hadn't done much of during the past couple of weeks.

"And I'll tell you something to cheer you up," Tod said. "If your Mark keeps on with his swimming at college next year, he might well be joining you for Nationals one day. He's a natural athlete. I think he could do well at any sport he puts his mind to. When we are in California, I'm going to have a talk with the UCLA coach to see if Mark can get on the team there."

"UCLA?" I squeaked. "You mean Mark could go to college in Los Angeles?"

He misunderstood my squeak. "Look, I know it will be tough for you to be separated, but it's bound to happen sometime."

"But, Tod, I'll be ecstatic if Mark goes to college in L.A.," I said and bounced out of his office. The silver lining had just twinkled out from under the dark cloud.

But other clouds were waiting to gather. When I thought about Mark and me, I thought in terms of next year, the year after that—but I had to deal with the present. Mark was now back in circulation at school. When I saw him in the halls, there were always kids hanging around him (including a lot of girls). I was glad for Mark, and I didn't have any reason to be jealous until one day I saw him coming out of a classroom, and the person he was talking to was Luanne—and they were walking very close together.

Luanne was the first to see me. She stopped short and said, "Oh, there's Jennie. Call me about it tonight, OK?" She hurried off.

Mark watched her go and grinned a bit sheepishly. "She wants me to help her with this chemistry project. We're doing this experiment in gases together."

"What fun," I said, trying not to sound like a clinging, jealous girlfriend. After all, Mark was entitled to help girls with chemistry projects, and if the girl happened to be Luanne Chapman, it surely couldn't matter. He had gotten over her long ago.

But I still felt uneasy, and Marilyn didn't make me feel any better. After workout she came into the shower next to mine. "Do you have any shampoo today? I forgot mine." I handed it to her and made a mental note that I kept Marilyn in shampoo.

"That Mark is getting to be a great backstroker," she said as she lathered up. "He's almost as good as you."

I nodded, not wanting to open my mouth and get soapy water in it.

"He's real cute, too," she said. "You're a

lucky girl. If you weren't such a good friend of mine, I'd steal him away from you."

The thought of Mark being stolen away by Marilyn made me smile. "You mean Miss Piggy?" he'd said when I had described her to him.

"But I'll tell you one thing." Marilyn lowered her voice, which wasn't necessary as the shower was splashing around us and we were the only ones in there. "There's someone else who's out to steal him away from you."

I tried to look calm.

"Luanne Chapman. I overheard her yesterday. She said she still thought he was the cutest boy in the school, and she wanted him back again. Then this other girl said, 'Well, you'd have to get rid of Jennie Webster first,' and Luanne just laughed and said, 'I don't think that would be the hardest thing in the world. I never could see what Mark saw in her.' "

"Thanks for the warning, Marilyn," I said. "But I'm not afraid of Luanne Chapman, and Mark doesn't think she's all that wonderful. He was badly hurt by her once."

"But you have to admit she's sexy," Marilyn said, wandering out of the shower, still clutching my shampoo bottle.

Of course I was worried about it. Of course I admitted that she was much prettier and more glamorous and sexier than I. But I had also heard Mark talk about her, about how she had come to visit him in the hospital, found out he couldn't play football again, and gone home in his best friend's car. Surely Mark couldn't ever forgive and forget something like that!

I knew that Marilyn was Oak Creek High's number-one gossip, and at least nine-tenths of the things she said weren't true, but I still brooded about it all the way home. Mark was sitting there right beside me in his car, talking on about this and that as if nothing was wrong. I kept telling myself not to be stupid. I wanted to come right out with it and ask him, but I couldn't bring myself to. Even when he said that I'd turned into Oscar the Grouch before his very eyes, I couldn't tell him what was wrong. So I just felt miserable and confused. That evening I picked at my dinner and skipped through my homework until finally, around nine o'clock, I decided to call him.

"Hello?" Josie answered the phone.

"Hi, is Mark there, please?"

"Is this Luanne again?" she asked immediately. I put the phone down without saying a word.

After that I paced around my room, calling Mark every bad word I could think of and punching a few stuffed animals. And then it came to me: no more Mark, no more reason to stay in Texas. And the world felt like a cold, lonely, and very empty place.

I cried myself to sleep. When I woke in the morning, my eyes looked all red and puffy. I had to splash cold water on them to make myself look normal. I told my mother that the chlorine had been bad. All the way through morning practice, I thought of confronting Mark, and right before school I lay in wait in the parking lot and grabbed him as soon as his car came to a halt.

"You and I have got to talk right now."

He looked very surprised. "What's wrong?"

"I think you know what."

He shook his head. "I wish I did. Have I done something?"

"Only dated Luanne Chapman without telling me. Oh, Mark—how could you?"

"Dating Luanne? What on earth gave you that idea?"

"I called your house last night and Josie picked up the phone. She said, 'Is this Luanne?' as if she expected her to be calling you late at night."

Mark was trying not to smile because I looked so mad. "You know y'all look awful cute when you are mad," he said in his fake southern accent.

"It's not funny!" I said. The anger was moving me to tears.

Mark put his arms around me. "I have to let you in on a little secret," he said. "My sister's greatest ambition is to be a cheerleader. And she thinks you are a poor substitute for Luanne as a girlfriend for me. Luanne called me last night about the chemistry project, and Josie was hopeful we were getting back together again. I suspect when she heard your voice, she was trying to stir things up a little."

I looked at him, trying to see from his face if he was lying or not.

"Don't you believe me?" he asked.

"I want to—but other people have said things to me, and she was with you the other day—"

Mark took my face in his hands. "Now listen to me, Jennie," he said tenderly. "You and I have got to trust each other. Just because Luanne might want to get back with me doesn't mean I want her back. I admit she's been chasing me pretty hard, but I'm not a dog who comes when he's called. I happen to be a person, and I happen to want you, not Luanne. Is that clear?"

I nodded.

"And I'll make you another promise. If ever it's over between us, I won't go behind your back and let you find out from someone else. There—now do you feel better?"

"Uh-huh."

"And I'll promise you one more thing."

"What's that?"

"When I get home, I'll personally murder that little sister of mine!"

Chapter 18

Thursday, March 12, and I was actually packing to go to Nationals. I was also playing a mental countdown game—this time tomorrow I will be on a plane, this time on Saturday I will have swum the hundred fly. This time next week it will all be over.

My mother came in with an armful of clean clothes, including her favorite dress. It was pale blue and frilly, and she was always trying to make me wear it.

"Shall I pack some of these for you?" she asked.

"Mom, I'll be in my suit or warm-up most of the time! And I won't need a dress!"

"There's bound to be a welcoming party or something. There always is—put on by the host club. You'll want to look nice for that."

"But, Mom, nobody will wear a dress to it. I'll take my Calvin Klein jeans and that nice blue velour top. OK?"

"You'll probably want to get married in jeans." My mother sighed and hung the dress back in the closet.

"How many suits are you taking?" she asked, fingering through the pile on the bed.

"A couple for warm-up plus my new meet suit."

"Why don't you take the blue Lycra, too, just in case you rip your meet suit or something?"

"Mom, I've been to a couple of thousand meets in my life, and I've never ripped a suit yet. Now please don't worry about me. I'll be fine. Honestly I will."

My mother sat down on the bed. "But I do worry about you, honey. I feel so bad that Daddy and I aren't coming with you. Sixteen is so very young to send someone halfway across the country by herself. But we just couldn't afford the plane fare for all three of us."

"I know, Mom. But please don't worry. Tod will take good care of me. He'll probably make me go to bed at seven-thirty and won't let me talk to strange boys."

"We've never been separated before. I suppose I had better get used to it. It won't be long till you're going off to college."

I came and sat down beside her. "I won't let you down at Nationals, Mom."

She took my hand, a little awkwardly because she wasn't usually a mother who went in for much physical contact. "Jennie, there's something I have to say to you. You may have thought that I've pushed you too hard or not cared enough about your feelings. You may have felt that I've lived only for your swimming or that I wanted you to succeed only to boost my own ego. That might be partly true, but that wasn't the main reason I was so hard on you. You see, I know what it's like to almost make it. If you almost get to the top but not quite, you spend the rest of your life wishing you had managed to make that last step."

Suddenly I understood a lot of things. "You must have felt pretty bad after that car crash, eh, Mom?"

She let out a long, tired sigh and then smiled at me as if she was glad I understood. "Pretty bad. The worst thing was that I wasn't even hurt. Just a concussion. But they kept me in the hospital for a few days of observation, and they wouldn't release me no matter how much I pleaded. And those few days were the Olympic trials. I kept telling myself that I'd make it next time. But of course by the next time I was too old and already married, and I'd quit swimming. That's what I wanted you to understand. If you don't make it now, you never will."

"I'll do my best, Mom," I said.

"I know you will, honey. Just remember while you are in California that—Oh, dear, there's the phone. I'll be right back."

I never did find out what I was to remember in California, because my mother came rushing back looking excited. "That was Daddy on the phone, and you'll never guess what happened. His old company called again, and they want him to open a branch here in Houston for them. He'll be his own boss and have his own office and everything. And it means you won't have to move after all."

I tried to smile. "Great," I said. What I thought was it was like living on the end of a yo-yo. Now we're staying here and Mark will probably go to UCLA.

I was glad now that I had kept Mark out of all these plans to move or not to move, to move me, to move him, to move back, and so on. He would have been just as confused by now as I was.

After school he came around to say goodbye. "Well, honeychild, I'm going to have a ball while you're gone, so don't you fret none 'bout me," he said, a teasing look on his face. "I'll be dating Luanne every night—"

I threw my stuffed elephant at him.

"I'll call you every evening," I said, "and tell you how I did that day."

"I might not be home," he said, looking mysterious. "But I suppose you can call if you like."

"Well, I'd better get used to calling you instead of seeing you," I said. "After all, next year you might be away at college somewhere."

"That's right," he said. "I'll be living it up in the big city. Different girl every night. I'll probably have forgotten all about you—"

I threw the pink snake at him.

"Do you mind not raining a zoo at me?"

I just had to get something straight. "Seriously, though, Mark, do you think you'll try for a swimming scholarship somewhere? Tod says he could probably get you into UCLA if you wanted to go."

Mark shook his head. "No, he already spoke to me about that. Why on earth would I want to go to California to college? Too many weird people come from there—no, don't throw the alligator! I thought about it, and I enjoy swimming, but just as a sport. I think I could be good, but I could never be great. I could never swim the way you do. You're a natural. I have to use all my power to keep on top of the water, but you seem to stay up there without any effort. So if I can't be the best, then I'll just do it for fun. After all, swimming isn't something you can do all your life—at twenty-one you're a has-been."

"So do you know what you'll do?"

"I think I've pretty much decided to take that art scholarship I won. And I think I'll probably go to the University of Texas at Austin. It's a neat campus with a good swim team, too, and I can drive home in a couple of hours."

"You can? You will?"

"You bet. And you can join me next year. After all, their swim team is one of the best, and it's getting better all the time."

"Oh, Mark—that will be great."

He looked at his watch. "Hey, I'd better be going. You have a plane to catch early in the morning, and I need all the rest I can get before those heavy dates with Luanne. Come over here and give me a bit of kissing practice."

I obliged, although the way he kissed, he didn't need any practice. Then he was gone, and I floated around the room. Mark at college in Austin. Me staying here with Tod. What a way to go off to Nationals! I felt like I could beat the entire world.

Chapter 19

"Aren't you going to finish that roll?" I asked Tod. I had already eaten my own lunch on the plane, and I was still starving. They made plane meals for tired business people, not swimmers in training.

"You can't still be hungry," Tod said. "The amount you eat, it's a wonder you don't go straight to the bottom."

"But, Tod, I'm nervous, and when I'm nervous, I always get hungry."

"Miss"—Tod grabbed a passing stewardess —"this young lady is on her way to swim in the National Championships, and your meal didn't give her enough calories. Can you find her a bite more?"

"A future Olympic champion, eh?" The stewardess gave me a big smile. "I'll see what I can do."

She disappeared into the galley. I sat there, crimson with embarrassment while people from the rows ahead turned around to see the future Olympic champion. Then the stewardess came back with another tray piled high with cheese and rolls and fruit and another slice of cake.

"Will this do?" she asked. "Good luck in your swimming."

I have to confess that I ate it all. It kept me busy until we landed in L.A. Then there was the cab ride to the hotel, and a great wave of homesickness poured over me. This was California, my state, with all those things I had taken for granted—the blue, cloudless skies, the hills always hovering in the background, the ocean, the flowers, and the palm trees. I almost rushed to the phone to call my folks and say, "Forget about opening the branch in Texas. Come on back home."

Instead I called Grandma as soon as I had settled into my hotel room. I wanted to call Mark, but of course he would still be at school.

"Is that my little Jennie?" came the gentle voice on the other end of the phone. "What are you doing in California?"

"I'm here for the Nationals at Mission Viejo."

"My, isn't that marvelous. What a clever girl you are. How long are you going to be here?"

"Four days."

"Oh, I might ask your aunt Sue if she'll drive me down to watch you."

"That would be great, Grandma."

"I think I'll get your cousin Angela to come, too. It would do her a world of good to see what normal, healthy girls do, instead of this dieting nonsense. Dieting and hair styles. That's all she can think of. And while you are here, why don't you come up and stay for a few days?"

"I'll have to ask my parents, but I'd really like to. I've missed you, Grandma."

"I miss you, too. But I'll be there cheering for you at your swimming one day. Whenever Aunt Sue can drive me. You swim well for Grandma now, won't you?"

Feeling comforted, I put down the phone. I was within reach of people I belonged to. My grandma might even be coming to watch me swim. That would mean I'd have someone in that big crowd to cheer for me.

At four o'clock we went down to the pool. It was quite an awe-inspiring sight—all sixteen lanes full, with the best swimmers in the country and on the edge a whole array of coaches—timing, shouting, whistling, comforting. I saw the Mission Viejo lane full of blue and yellow suits; their coach was watching them all like a hawk. I couldn't help feeling sorry for poor old Tod, who only had me instead of a laneful of swimmers, and I was determined that he'd be proud of me.

He put a hand on my shoulder. "OK, kiddo. Get in there and do your stuff. How about a thousand warm-up, then we'll go over to the sprint lane for some sprints."

I looked for a fairly empty lane, but there didn't seem to be one. I could hardly lower myself into the middle of another team's workout. I felt like the new girl at school and stood there gaping.

Suddenly a blond head emerged from the water below me, and a giant hand waved.

"Hey, Jennie! Good to see you. Get in and work out with us." It was Rick, my former rival and car-pool buddy, now another foot taller by the look of him. I got in gratefully and swam along slowly beside Rick.

"I kept looking out for you," he said. "How have you been?"

"Oh, fine."

"How's Texas?"

"OK, thanks."

"We miss you," he said. "Now I don't have any heels to grab."

"I miss you all, too."

"What are you swimming?"

"Both the fly events, hundred free and hundred back. How about you?"

"All the two hundreds, five hundred free, and four hundred I.M."

"Hey, you must have improved," I said a little grudgingly. "I remember you only had one qualifying time last year."

"Yes, well, I'm just coming into my prime now. You wait till you see me in action tomorrow."

"Jennie! Quit talking and get moving!" I heard Tod's voice boom out.

Rick glanced up at Tod. "He still as mean as ever?"

"Even meaner," I said and started my warm-up.

There were a couple of other boys in my lane who were from my old team. I felt much better now that I knew somebody at the meet. The workout felt good, and I was feeling quite pleased with myself.

As soon as I had dried off, I called Mark, just to let him know I'd arrived safely. Seven o'clock here meant nine o'clock in Texas. I had worked it out. His mother answered.

"I'm sorry, hon. Mark's not here right now," she said. "Yes, I'll tell him you called."

I put back the receiver very slowly. My first night away and he was already out somewhere? And with whom?

That evening there was a big barbecue for all the swimmers. A couple of girls did wear dresses, but they were in the minority. I was glad my mother and the frilly dress were two thousand miles away.

I hung around the doorway like a little star-struck kid, recognizing the big names in swimming and feeling very small and insignificant. I could hardly believe that tomorrow morning I would be swimming against them.

I felt so insecure that I needed an extra helping of spareribs and potato salad. Besides being hungry, it gave me something to do so that I didn't have to stand there looking lost.

Tod came up to me. "Not eating again?"

"These spareribs are delicious. Have one?"

He took one. "Having a good time?"

"Frankly, it's all a bit much for me," I had to admit. "All these big names walking around with plates of spareribs as if they were just ordinary people."

Tod laughed. "I shouldn't be surprised if after tomorrow you weren't one of those names yourself and people will be saying about you, 'Look how she eats spareribs like an ordinary person.' "

"Oh, Tod!"

"Come on, I'll introduce you to some of your big names if you like."

But before we could move, a tall man with a mustache who looked familiar came up to us and shook hands with Tod. Then he turned to me. "A little bird tells me you might be coming to join us—is that right?"

I wondered for a moment where I had seen him before. Then I remembered that he was the Mission Viejo coach.

"Er—actually I've decided to stay on with Tod in Texas for the next few months," I stammered.

"That's our bad luck," he said. "Good luck tomorrow. I expect you to win that hundred fly."

Then he patted me on the shoulder and left. I don't remember much about the rest of the evening after that. It went by in a daze. All I could think of was that this famous man recognized me and even wanted me on his team. I felt like the biggest celebrity of them all.

When I got home, I was going to call Mark again. Then I saw that it was ten o'clock here, which would make it midnight in Texas, so I decided I had better not wake his family. I wondered if he'd tried to call me. I wondered where he had been.

"I'll call first thing in the morning," I decided.

Next morning I opened my eyes to the half darkness of a strange room. For a moment I listened to the distant hum of traffic on the freeway, trying to remember where I was. Then it hit me like a great punch in the stomach.

"Today is the day. Hundred fly this morning!" It seemed unfair that my best race should also be my first. At least I could have wasted the hundred free or hundred back getting into the swing of things. The heats were at ten-thirty in the morning. Then, if I made finals, those started at seven tonight. A long day ahead.

I looked at my watch. Six o'clock California time. That meant eight o'clock in Texas. I dialed Mark's number. I would probably wake him out of his Saturday-morning sleep, but I didn't care. The phone rang four times before it was answered.

"Hello?"

"Hi, Mark?"

"This is Mark's dad. Who's calling, please?"

"Oh, Mr. Waverly. This is Jennie. I'm calling from California."

"Well, hi there, Jennie. How are you?"

"Fine, thank you."

"Ready for the big day?"

"I hope so. Listen, can I speak to Mark, please? I may not have time to call him later, and I missed him last night."

"Well, honeychild, the fact is—he's not here right now."

"He's not?"

"No—I guess he went out real early this morning."

There was a pause during which I heard the humming of our long-distance line. "I'm sorry, Jennie," he said. "I'll tell him you called just as soon as he gets in. Good luck in your race, y'hear?"

"Thank you, Mr. Waverly. Bye."

I had a sinking feeling as I put down the phone. How could Mark not be there at eight o'clock on a Saturday morning—unless—unless he went somewhere last night and didn't come back. His mother had sounded a little flustered or embarrassed last night, and his father had sounded this morning as if he were not quite telling the whole truth.

Oh, Mark, I thought. *You wouldn't—would you? Not go out somewhere, to an all-night party or do something even worse, the first night I was away?* I tried not to believe it, but I kept thinking about Luanne waiting for this moment when I was safely two thousand miles away. I remembered what she had said: "Getting rid of Jennie Webster won't be the hardest thing in the world."

I ran several scripts through the private movie theater in my brain. Scripts that began with Luanne calling Mark and sounding desperate about her chemistry homework; Luanne missing her ride home and telling him he was the only one she knew with a car; Luanne inviting him to go to a movie with the gang, only when he got there there wasn't any gang.

All this succeeded in doing was to make me feel more nervous on an already nervous day. I was so jittery, in fact, that when I went down to breakfast I ordered cornflakes with peaches on them, then two eggs, sausage, hash browns, and pancakes, and ate it all.

"Cheer up," Tod said as we rode to the pool.

"Hmmmpp."

"You're going to do fine."

"Hmmmpp."

"I get the feeling you don't want to talk."

"Hmmmph."

He must have gotten home by now, I thought as I changed in the locker room. *I'll call once more.* I found the nearest pay phone. Armed with enough change to reach Texas, I dialed. This time no one answered.

I warmed up and felt pretty good. The water felt just right, and my arms felt loose and light as they came out of the water. I saw from the program that I was seeded third, and that made me feel even better. If only I could just talk to Mark, everything would be perfect. So after warm-up I called again.

One ring—answer somebody.

Two rings—come on, pick up the phone.

Three rings—Mark, I command you, pick up that phone right now.

Four rings—come on, Mark, please, please answer the phone now... please, please....

After seven rings I convinced myself that he was not going to answer. I went back to the locker room. It was now deserted, everyone else having already changed and gone out to do their thing. I sat on the bench and stared at nothing. Why did they make locker rooms such gloomy places? Why no windows? Why gray or green lockers. This needs Mark to paint a mural—flowers and birds and blue sky and—

"Are you swimming the hundred fly?" a voice beside me asked.

I jumped a mile, shaken out of my daydream. "Yes, yes I am."

"Then you better get out there. They've already handed out cards, and they're on the final heat of the two hundred breast," she said.

I grabbed my towel and ran. Tod pounced on me as soon as I came to the pool area. "Where the hell have you been? I've been searching all over—you scared the hell out of me. Now get down there to those blocks and don't forget everything I've taught you. It's a sprint—you're not saving anything, you're going to explode off those blocks and give it all you've got for four lengths. Come hard into your turns and give a powerful kick as you come out; when you see the red lane line on the final length, just put your head down and go. Don't forget the race might be decided on hundredths of a second, so that fast touch really counts. You got all that?"

"You know I have. You've said it millions of times before."

He gave me a hug. "Go out there and win, Jennie."

Then I walked, all alone, down to the blocks. The loudspeaker was blaring out, "Event seven, ladies one-hundred-yard butterfly. Heat one to the blocks, please. In lane one . . ."

Eight swimmers climbed onto the blocks.

The starter's gun sounded, and they hit the water. They all looked incredibly fast. How could this be the slowest heat? There were five heats altogether and, because of international seeding rules, you put your fastest swimmers in lane four, next fastest in lane five, and so on. I would be swimming in heat three, lane four. This seeding is hard on the top seeds. It means you are always swimming at the top of a pyramid. You have nobody to pace you, no one to try to beat in the heats. It's only in the finals that you come up against the swimmers who are better than you.

Heat two was over. The girls dragged themselves from the water and watched the scoreboard for their times, looking happy or sad depending on what numbers were flashed up beside their names.

Then it came: "Heat three to the blocks, please." I took off my warm-up jacket and shook out my arms and legs. I could hear a lot of cheering coming from the beachers.

"In lane one, from the Santa Clara Swim Club . . ." Loud cheers.

"In lane two, from Amberjax . . ." More cheers.

"In lane three, from Mission Viejo . . ." Loudest cheers yet. Lots of supporters for the home team.

"In lane four, swimming for the South Texas Marlins, Jennie Webster."

I stepped up onto my block. Polite cheers from the crowd. Except for one particularly loud voice.

"Yeah, Jennie! Go get 'em, girl!"

I looked over to my left in utter amazement. Had I imagined it? Could I have imagined it? Then I saw him—Texas hat, grin, and all. He waved like crazy and blew me a kiss. No wonder he hadn't answered my phone calls. How could he when he was on a plane chasing me halfway across the United States?

"Ladies, this is the one-hundred-yard butterfly," said the starter. "Take your marks."

My whole body became tense—a bullet waiting to be shot from a gun barrel. Mark had come all this way to watch me swim, and I was not going to let him down.

Even before the starter's gun had died away, I exploded outward and hardly noticed the water as it came up to meet me. Watch out, America. Here comes the new Nationals champion!

Sweet
Dreams

hard-working Jeff and handsome, budding rock star Skip. Which will make her happy?

LITTLE SISTER by Yvonne Greene

Cindy's beautiful older sister, Christine, gets all the cute boys. Cindy just can't win. Then she meets Ron, the best actor in high school. This time Cindy is Number One. But when Christine is chosen to play opposite Ron in the school production of *Romeo and Juliet,* Cindy must prove that she's not second best in Ron's heart.

CALIFORNIA GIRL by Janet Quin-Harkin

Jennie is an outsider in her new Texas home. She is determined to be an Olympic swimmer, but in Texas, all anyone cares about is football. Mark was a high school football star . . . until his accident. But Jennie has fallen in love with his artistic soul and secretly enters his drawings in a contest. Overnight, Mark is a star again. But he may be leaving Jennie behind. Is Jennie losing her love *and* her Olympic dream?

GREEN EYES by Suzanne Rand
(*coming in December*)

Dan is one of the most popular boys in school and really cares for Julie. But every time Julie sees Dan so much as talk to another girl, she becomes hopelessly jealous. Then Dan's old girlfriend returns and Julie is convinced that Dan is seeing her again, though Dan assures her he's not. Will Julie let her jealousy ruin the best relationship she's ever had?

THE THOROUGHBRED by Joanna Campbell
(*coming in December*)

Things have always come easily for Maura—her parents are rich, she's pretty, and she's brilliant at horseback riding. Then Maura meets Kevin, a dark, handsome boy, and falls in love for the first time. But Kevin wants too much from her too soon and she's scared. Feeling rejected, Kevin decides to show Maura up in a riding competition. But Maura is determined to win even if she loses her first love doing so.

(*Read all of these great Sweet Dreams romances, available wherever Bantam Books are sold.*)